I'm Still Wifey

a novel

by

Kiki Swinson

I'm Still Wifey

For information address:

Melodrama Publishing
P. O. Box 522
Bellport, New York 11713-0522

Web address: www.melodramapublishing.com
e-mail: melodramapub@aol.com
Author's e-mail address: kikis7673@yahoo.com

Library of Congress Control Number: 2005936565

ISBN 0-9717021-5-2
First Edition

Dedication

From the heart I got to shout out my two bad a#@ kids….**Shaquira & Lil J.** Once again mommy is on the grind trying to get that paper, because I know y'all aren't going to have it any other way, which is why I want to thank you two for keeping me focused.

To my baby—**Mr. Karl Blackstock—aka—Black**, in such a short time you have opened my eyes and heart to unlimited possibilities and I want to thank you for that. But most importantly, I want to thank you for your effortless way of keeping a smile on my face with your sense of humor. It feels good to have you on my team. Oh & your joint, **"Guilty Pleasures,"** will be hitting the bookstores real soon. **Believe that!!!!!!!!!**

Acknowledgements

To my **Lord & Savior Jesus Christ**, who stands in the gap for me on a daily basis. Boy, am I grateful for that. But, most importantly blessed.

To my publisher, **Crystal Lacy Winslow**—who happens to be a well accomplished business woman & **best selling author** of **Love, Life & Loneliness, The Criss Cross**. Once again you had my back, so I want to thank you for believing in me & my work even though I have a crew of haters throwing salt at me every chance they got.... *(They just don't know that, **God don't like ugly!**)*

My father, Loyd Drew is the man. I love you very much & want to thank you for all your spiritual & moral support. Oh & I haven't forgotten about you Onita. You're in the family now. So, treat my dad right!!!!

To my mom Deborah White, I love you & thanks for creating a literary genius. And to my grandmother—Clara P. Swinson, you know that I could not have done this without your support and your prayers. So, thanks for staying on those knees & know that I will always love you!!!!

To my baby sister Sunshine Swinson, girl I know you would have killed me if I didn't give you your own paragraph, so here it is: Thanks so much for your constructive criticism & your vision when it came to the development of this book. You are a reading fanatic, that's why I value your opinions. So, do you still want your car painted girlfriend? (*smile*) I love you baby sis!!!!

To my brothers, Eugene & Jamon Swinson—I love you both too death. And even though we have our hectic lives to lead, I just wish that there was a way we could spend more time together; besides at the family reunions. (*smile*)

My cousin Xyamara Hines & her man Pie, I love you both too. Y'all are my family& I'm going to always have your back!!! So, keep your heads up!

To my big brother Joe Cameron, there's so much I want to thank you for, but I'll probably have to type up about five more pages. So, I'm gonna keep it short and say, that you're a good man, a good provider for your children, a good brother to your sisters & a damn good friend to me.

Always coming to my rescue and I love you like you're blood. So, don't you ever forget that!

Hey, Ms. Dominique Mitchell. You know you were next on my list of folks to acknowledge. You also know how far our friendship stretches back to the early-eighties. And how the chicks from junior high use to hate on us? Yeah, those were the times. But, look at us now! Ole' Ladies, sitting back watching our own daughters hanging out with each other trying to pull the same trips on us. But, it ain't flying over my head! *(smile)*….Anyway, there's a permanent place in my heart for you. I love you sis!!!! I love you uncle Leo, aunt Sharon, Tommy, Francisca & Lil L-L!!!!

To my auntie & diva—Mrs. Karen Johnson, once again you gave me the go-ahead with your seal of approval after reading the 1st draft of this book. I trust your judgment 100%, because you are as real as it gets. And most importantly, I love you! So, put your coat on & let's get out of Virginia Beach for a while…It's on me! (smile)

To my best friend Letitia Carrington, who I can say has my best interest in heart. You and I have been friends for over fifteen years now & I cherish every one of those days up to this very moment. What can I say other than I love you…..? Also, congrats…to you & Herman on having that beautiful baby boy... (Jaden). He's so cute! Yeah, he's going to be terrible just like my son Lil J! (smile)

To my sidekick, Malika Foster, girl it seems like the older your ass gets the better you look! Yeah, you know you got it going on. Niggaz is loving your red ass! But, I love you even more because you are a damn good friend to me. Not only that, I want to thank you for holding me down on all my book touring trips because without you, I would not have had so many men coping my books. They see you & go bananas! (smile) I love you too Aunt Nancy & Hope!

To home girl Pookie-aka-Vandelette Ware, I'm just a little lost for words when I think about how instrumental you've been in my life. You are a very beautiful woman & tremendous blessing to everyone who crosses your path. I love you!!!!!

To Tiffany Hoyt, I know you're constantly traveling across miles of bumpy road, but you're a strong woman so you'll get pass it all real soon. Keep your head up!!!

To my sister's in crime, Kimberlie Flemmings (in Charlotte, NC) & Iona Christian (Brooklyn, NY), I love you both so much for always having my back & keeping it real. I couldn't ask for anything better than that. Believe that we will be friends for life.

To Joan Chisholm -aka- Joan, you have an unconditional love for me, which is why I treat you like my older sister. I love you, Ma & that ackee & salt fish you be hooking up for me!!!

To my other family & friends like: my aunt Brenda Byrd & her husband Michael Byrd, my cousin Michael Byrd –aka-Gee & his beautiful wife Pam, & to my other cousin Michael Byrd –aka- Ant., my cousin Duke Woodley, my labelmate Amaleka McCall **(author of A Twisted Tale of Karma)** girl you just don't know, but you're on your way. To my friend & Essence Bestselling author Treasure E. Blue **(Harlem Girl Lost),** thanks for the many encouraging words you gave me. Who would have thought that you would be right after all? Thanks for everything. Also to my girl Yoni Wyatt, Tabitha (out of N.Y.), my girl "Flo" (out of N.Y. driving that *hot 3-series BMW*), Paula 'Nikki' Bell, Chekesha 'Cha-Cha' Carter, Ina Mcgriff, Sharney –aka- Sunshine, Dee Dee Smalls, Dana & Katrina Brown, Chiquita Coleman, Melissa White –aka- Missy Fro, Shawntae Gatling, Naomi T. Barnes, my neighbor Tommy, his roommate Tim & Danielle Mills, my manicurist Kelly @ (Body & Soul Nail Spa), my favorite supporters Linda, Trish, Ron & Patrick @ (Waldenbooks in Military Circle Mall), all people in P-town, Norfolk, Va. Beach & the rest of the Tidewater area. To my girl Michelle @ Hair Visions (in Berkley), my girl "Twiggy" @ Jazzy Hair & Nails, my hair stylist Lori @ Beautiful Reflections (in Norfolk), my girl "V" @ Exotic Glamour Hair Care (in Norfolk), my ladies @ Mane Image, Jeremiah @ Hair Art, Fred @ Hair Divas & to the rest of the stylist who continue to support me like: my girl Gayette & her sister who can hook up some nails & rest of the crew.

To all my people on lock: Leshawn Pullie (Petersburg Camp), Kevin Jones–aka-Ron (Petersburg), Lee Spears –aka Reggie (Petersburg Camp), Leonard Marshall–aka-Bolo (Petersburg), Lil Bill (Petersburg Camp), Shedrick Wilson–aka- Pork-n-Bean (Lawrenceville, Va.), John Davis – aka- Smoke (Norfolk City Jail), Lucion Freeman, Tony Harris, Lil Mook, Kesha Stuart –aka- Lil Mama, Montal Smith –aka- Tizzy, my cousin Jerry Atkinson –aka- Kut, Shawn Hooper, Lisa Banks (Dublin FCI), Renea

Darby (Coleman FCI), & to Ervin "E" Smith (hurry up & come on home, my nephew needs his father). And not to forget all the ladies who played a part in my life when I had to break my bid up & do time at Danbury FCI, Butner Camp & Alderson Camp. And to all the real men holding it down doing their state & federal bids. Keep your heads up soldiers!!!

R.I.P to: Alvin Hooper (who was like a father to me), my cousin Cardy Woodley, Faye Gatling, "Big Shah" Mcfarland, Wink & Randy, Butter (from Norfolk), Derrick "Tilley," Steven Hughes –aka- Lil Steve, Trevor Casper & last but not least my dear friend Ronald G. Luper. I truly miss you all!

IT AIN'T OVER

Can you believe it? After all the planning I did to leave my husband Ricky to run off with Russ, it backfired on me. It has been two-and-a-half months since the whole thing went down. Now I'm sitting here all alone, in my hair shop, thinking about what I am going to do about this baby I'm carrying.

Rhonda and Nikki both didn't believe me when I told them that I was pregnant by Russ. But after I pulled out a calendar and counted back the days from the last time we were together, it finally registered through their thick skulls.

"So, what cha' gon' do about it?" Rhonda asked me the day I got the results from a pregnancy test about a month ago. The first thing that came out of her mouth was for me to get an abortion since I ain't gon' have a baby daddy. God knows where he is. But I told her that was the furthest thing from my mind because whether I had Russ in my life or not, I was gon' have this baby. And then she said, "Well, what would you do if he found out you're pregnant and wants to come back with a whole bunch of apologies and shit?"

I told her that shit ain't gon' happen because first of all, Russ ain't gon' find out I'm pregnant 'cause ain't nobody gon' know I'm pregnant by him. And second, after that stunt he pulled on me to rob me for my dough, I know he ain't gon' never show his face around this way ever again. He would be a fool to. I mean, he don't know if I told Ricky that he robbed me or not. So to play it cool, he's gon' do like any other greasy-ass nigga would do after they pull a stick-up move, and that is to disappear. And even though he thinks he got away with it, he hasn't. 'Cause whether Russ knows it or not, karma is coming for his ass. And what will give me much pleasure is to be able to see it hit 'em.

Hopefully my day will come very soon.

Back at my place, which is a step down from my ol' two-story house, I decided to pop myself a bag of popcorn and watch my favorite show, *America's Next Top Model*. Afterward, I began to straighten things up around my two bedroom, two-bath condo until my telephone started ringing.

"Hello," I said without looking at the CallerID.

"Whatcha doing?" Rhonda wanted to know.

"I was just dusting the mantel over my fireplace."

"Girl, sit your butt down. 'Cause if my memory serves me, I do remember you being on your feet all day today."

"I'm fine. But what I wanna know is, why you didn't come back to work today?"

Rhonda sighed heavily and said, "Kira, if I could kill Tony

and get away with it, I would do it."

"What happened now?"

"Girl, I caught this nigga talking to some hoe named Letisha on his cell phone."

"Where was he at?"

"He was in the bathroom, sitting on the fucking toilet, taking a shit."

I laughed at Rhonda's comment and asked her what happened next.

"Well, before I busted in on him and smacked him upside his damn head with my shoe, I stood very quiet in the hallway right outside our bedroom and heard this bastard telling that hoe how much he missed her and that he was going to get his hair cut at the barbershop. And right after I heard him say that, that's when I went off."

"So, what did he do?"

"He couldn't do shit with his pants wrapped around his ankles. So, he just sat there and took all them blows I threw at his ass. And then when he dropped his cell phone, I hurried up and snatched it right off the floor and cussed that bitch out royally."

"And what did she say?"

"I ain't let her say shit. 'Cause after I told her who I was and that if I ever caught her in Tony's face, she was gonna get fucked up, I hung up."

"So, what was Tony doing while you was going off on that hoe?"

"Trying to hurry up and wipe his ass, so he can get up from the toilet and I guess take his phone back. But as soon as the bastard stood up to flush the stool, I threw his phone right up against the wall as hard as I could and broke that bad boy in about ten little pieces."

I laughed again and said, "Damn girl! That's some shit I

used to do."

"Well, jackass didn't see it coming. So, it made it all the better."

"Where's he at now?"

"In the kitchen helping Ryan with his homework."

"So, did he ever go out and get his hair cut?"

"Hell nah. Shit, he knew better."

"Well, what kind of lies did he tell you about everything that happened?"

"Girl, that nigga ain't gon' volunteer no information. All he had to say was that I was crazy as hell. And then he went on about his damn business."

"Rhonda," I said before I sighed, "I know you're sick and tired of going through all that bullshit! Because I sure was when Ricky was on the streets."

"Hey wait," Rhonda interjected, "I forgot to tell you that he called the shop today while you was at lunch."

"Did you accept the call?"

"Yeah. But we only talked for a few minutes."

"What did he say?"

"He just wanted to know where you was and when was you coming in. So, I told him that you wasn't. And that's when he asked me to call you on three-way. But I told him the three-way call thing wasn't working."

"I bet he got real mad, didn't he?"

"Hell yeah!"

"So, what did he say after that?"

"Nothing but to tell you he called. And for me to tell you to come down to the county jail and see him before the U.S. Marshal picks him up and takes him off to the Federal Holding Facility in Oklahoma, because he has something very important to talk with you about."

"Well, he should already know that it ain't gon' happen. But,

I am wondering what he's got so important to talk to me about."

"Girl, he's just probably saying that so he can get you to come down and see him."

"Yeah. You probably right," I agreed.

"Well, are you going to ever tell him that you're pregnant by Russ?" Rhonda blurted out of the blue.

"Nope. It ain't none of his damn business. All he needs to focus on is signing those divorce papers my lawyer is getting ready to send his ass."

"So, you're serious about that, huh?"

"You damn right!" I commented and then I said, "I'm gonna get that nigga outta my life once and for all, so I can move on."

"Look, I understand all that. But I wouldn't let his ass get off that easy. Because the next time he calls the shop, I would make it my business to wreck his muthafucking ego and tell him, '*Yeah nigga, while you was running around behind my back with Sunshine's stinking ass, I was fucking your boy Russ right in your bed. And I just found out that I'm pregnant by him.*'"

"Oh my God! That'll kill him!"

"That's the idea," Rhonda told me.

I said, "Girl, that nigga gon' try and come through the phone after I tell him some shit like that."

"Well, no need to worry 'bout that. 'Cause it ain't gon' happen." Before I could comment, she told me to hold on because somebody was beeping in on her other line. When she clicked over, it got real quiet. But just like that, she was right back on the line and said, "Hey girl, one of Tony's homeboys is on the other end trying to holler at him. So, let me call you back."

"A'ight," I told her. Then we both hung up.

CHOICE TO MAKE

"Hello, ladies," is the first thing I said when I walked though the front door of my shop.

"Hey," everybody replied in unison.

"Anybody called me?" I asked loud enough for Rhonda and my other two stylists, Porsha and April, to hear me.

Porsha answered, "Nah, I don't think so." Then she went outside the shop to smoke a cigarette. She's a cool girl and really pretty, looking like Jada Pinkett-Smith's twin. But of course, she's a new jack. She started working here two weeks after I came back. She's also very young. She says she's twenty-one, but she acts like she's about sixteen sometimes, especially when it comes to cleaning up behind herself. Rhonda gets on her all the time about keeping her station area clean. I'm always sitting back, watching. Oh, but I did step in the mix of things a couple of times when booth rent was due. Porsha kept giving Rhonda the runaround, so I stepped up to the plate and that hoe handed over the dough. Recently, it has become clear that the two don't like each other, so it won't be long before she's outta here. Now April, on the other hand, is crazy. I mean, buck wild, but Rhonda and I know where she's coming from. She's your average-looking chick with a tabletop ass. Mad cats be trying to holler at her. But once they find out she's got a house full of kids, they do not stick around long at all. That's why she's always hanging out at a nightclub. Her favorite spot is Sugar Ray's off Military Highway. And like a devoted patron, she's there every time the doors open. But once that part of her life is put to a halt she's right back here, whipping up the fly-ass hairstyles. "Oh yeah," April broke out and said, "Your client Ms. Gladys and her daughter been here."

"Did she say she was coming back?" I asked as I began to plug in all of my curling irons and hot plate.

"Yeah. She said she was just going to go and get something to eat."

"A'ight," I said and then I signaled one of my clients who was sitting in the waiting room to walk over to the washbowl.

"Come on, Tina," I instructed her. "Whatcha getting done?" I asked her once she was standing directly in front of me.

"I want you to make me a short wig with a Mohawk."

"What kind of hair did you get?"

"Two packs of twenty-seven pieces," she told me. I told her to sit down and that's when I started working on her hair, which didn't take long at all to hook up. Once she was out of the way, I hammered away at my other five clients for the day and before I knew it I was done and out of the door.

From the shop, I decided to go home but I needed something to put on my stomach, so I stopped at the Taco Bell off the corner of Virginia Beach Boulevard and Independence. To my surprise, I saw Ricky's baby mama Frances standing in line with some ol' cornball-ass nigga, ordering herself some food. Now from the looks of things, nothing about her had changed in the past two months. She still held the crown for the " Knock off Queen." As I stood and watched her parade around this guy, with her jacked-up weaved hairdo, wearing a pair of Crest jeans, some ordinary-looking shirt, and a fake-ass Gucci bag draped over her bony-ass shoulders.

On the other hand, her boyfriend was cute and he looked all right. Even though them brand new Lebron James sneakers he had on were a year old. And now that I could see him a little closer, he was definitely a new breed. His mannerisms told me that he had to be in the military. Now I say this because street niggas wear their jeans at least two to four sizes bigger than their norm. But this cat's attire fit him to a tee. Yeah, 'cause the more and more I think about it this cat gotta be a boat boy. Street cats don't pull all their dough outta their pocket at once unless their asses is being robbed. So, I cannot see this dummy being nothing else.

Right after their food was handed to them, they both turned around to leave. Now, only after taking just one step, Frances noticed that I was standing only a few feet away from them. And I've got to admit that her facial expression turned really sour. She wasn't trying to hide it either. But it didn't faze me at all because the closer she got to me, the bigger my fake smile got.

"Hello, stranger," I said in a cheerful way. But she didn't crack a smile when she said, "I heard you did some foul ass shit!"

"What cha' talking about?" I wanted to know.

"I'ma be in the car," her male friend interjected before she could speak. As he walked out of Taco Bell, I asked her again what was she talking about?

"Don't play stupid," she replied sarcastically.

"What the fuck you mean, *'don't play stupid?'*" I snapped back.

She stepped closer to me and said, "One of my peoples just told me they saw you coming outta the FBI Building right before Ricky got picked up from the Feds."

Ahh shit! I said to myself. *Now what the fuck am I gonna do now?* My thoughts continued as I stood in front of this project chick.

"So, it must be true."

"Oh no, honey. That information you got is totally false."

"Yeah, that's what your mouth say. But I know my girl Freda ain't lying, 'cause, she cleans up the building right across the street from the FBI building, so I know she saw you."

"Look, I don't give a fuck what your friend Freda said. I know I haven't ever been in the FBI building, much less went in there right before Ricky got locked up. So what you and your friend need to do is find somebody else to talk about. Because right now, you don't know what the hell you're talking about."

"Oh, I know what I'm talking about," she retaliated in a hostile way. "And as soon as Ricky calls me again, I'm gon' tell him that your trifling ass is a fucking snitch!"

"Look, bitch! I ain't no snitch! So you better watch your mouth!"

"And if I don't?" Frances responded intending to press my buttons.

I put my hands up in her face and said, "Let me go before I give your ass a beat down in here."

I headed out of the restaurant. But Frances wasn't trying

to hear that. This hoe started walking behind me, brewing up more commotion, saying, "Yeah, you're doing right by carrying your stuck-up ass out of here. Because if you think you can beat my ass, then you got to be crazy."

I stopped in my tracks and turned towards her. "Frances, all jokes aside, you don't want none of me. Because whether you know it or not, I've been holding plenty of shit back for a very long time, trying to keep from killing you, bitch! And this was done on the strength of my husband because he asked me to keep the peace at a good level so he can see his grown-ass daughter."

"Bitch!" Frances screamed, cutting me off in mid-sentence. "Don't be bringing my daughter in this ."

She threw a punch at me and it landed right over my left eye.

"You fucking bitch!" I screamed as loud as I could after feeling the sting of the blow. I didn't stop there because after I pulled my hand away from my eye to see if it was bleeding, I jumped dead on her stinky ass.

I hit her ass back as hard as I could with my left fist. I hit her with this hand because I wanted to leave the imprint of the huge rocks in my wedding ring on her face. This ended up becoming a beautiful sight as I watched the blood pour down her face. But since I didn't get enough satisfaction outta that, I grabbed Frances by the shirt and slammed her down onto this red car parked right next to where we were standing. You should've seen her trying to throw them weak-ass punches at me. But, them little-ass blows didn't faze me at all. To try to get the best of her, I grabbed her by her throat and began to choke the hell outta her.

"Yeah! You thought you was gon' beat my ass, huh? But I fooled the hell outta your trick ass!" I screamed.

"Bitch, you ain't doing shit but holding me down! You ain't

got no fighting game for real," Frances managed to say while I kept a tight grip around her neck.

Now, I ain't gon' front, this chick had balls. I mean, here I was, standing over her, trying to choke the daylights out of her and she's still talking shit to me.

At that moment I figured out that the only way I was going to get her to shut up was to beat the brakes off her ass. That's when I took one of my hands from around her neck and tried to bless that ass right across her again, but her punk-ass boyfriend came from outta nowhere and grabbed me by my damn arm.

"You better get the fuck off me!" I screamed on him as nasty as I could.

"Nah, home girl, you need to get off her," he replied aggressively.

While this nigga had my attention for a bit, Frances reached up and grabbed a handful of my hair and began to twist it in a fucking knot.

Now I had just got my shit sewed in, so you know I wasn't prepared for this. So, to keep this hoe from pulling all my damn hair out, I tried to lower my head. But it seemed like the more I gave in, the more she tried to pull it. And that's when I said, "Frances, let go of my hair!"

"Get off me first," she demanded.

"Yeah, get off of her," her boyfriend told me once again as he continued to hold onto my arm. I snatched my arm right out of his hand and told him, "Don't grab me no muthafucking more! Now, tell her to let my hair go and I'll get off of her."

"Bitch, you must think I'm stupid!" Frances commented with a smirk on her face. And from that point, I knew I wouldn't be able to get her to let go of my hair unless I got off her first. I told her, "Look, I'ma get off you, but you gon' have to let go of my hair at the same time."

"Just get off her. She's gon' let your hair go," her boyfriend said again.

"Look, I'm not talking to you. I'm talking to her," I replied sarcastically as my head lay hunched over. And then out of nowhere I heard somebody yell out, "The police is coming!" I scrambled to my feet, giving Frances room to move. But she still had my hair gripped really tight in the palm of her hand.

"Look, I'm off you, so let my hair go," I told Frances as calmly as I knew how. Even so, I knew she had the upper hand and could steal a couple of punches off me at will. But before she could say or do anything, the police siren got louder. And that's when her boyfriend said, "Frances, you better come on before they roll up on you and find out you got a warrant."

And just like that she let go of my hair. Then she and her boyfriend jumped into his car and drove off like they had just robbed a bank.

The police rolled up in the parking lot a few seconds later, and they drove up with force like they was gon' really do something. But I wasn't worried at all because the one person who could've gotten me locked up jetted off. So, I just stood there patting my hair. And then I started re-adjusting my clothes as I watched both police officers walk towards me.

"Ma'am, are you one of the two women reported to have been fighting out here?" the black male officer asked me.

"Yes, I am," I told him as I combed my hair with my fingers.

"So, where is the other woman?"

"She got in a car with some guy and left."

"What color and make was this vehicle?" the white officer stepped in and asked as he began to write what I was telling him down on his note pad.

"I don't know what kind of car it was, but I do remember that it was dark-blue."

"Did you know who this woman was?" The black officer wanted to know.

"Yeah, I know her."

"Okay. Well, tell us why the altercation started?" the black officer's questions continued.

Now, before I began to explain why me and Frances started fighting, I looked behind me and noticed a crowd of people standing around, watching me talking to the police, which was kind of funny. I cracked a little smile and that's when the white officer asked me, "What's so funny?"

"Nothing."

"Well, are you going to tell us what happened?" he continued.

"Look officers, I don't mean no disrespect. But, all I was doing was standing in line waiting to order my food and that's when that project chick got in my face and started talking madness."

"What is her name?" the white officer wanted to know.

"Frances."

"So, what happened next?" the white officer's questions continued.

"Well, since I wasn't trying to hear nothing she had to say, I just walked away from her. But she followed me outside to right here where we're standing. And then she hit me so we started *knucking*."

"Where did she hit you?" the black officer jumped back in and asked.

"Right here above my eye." I pointed to my left eye.

"Would you like for us to call the paramedics?" the black officer continued.

"Nah. I'm straight. I mean it ain't nothing but a lil scratch."

"Well, do you wanna file charges against her?" the white officer interjected.

"I'm not sure. Can I think about it?"

"Well, are you sure you wanna do that? Because we can start the paperwork now," the black officer intervened.

"Look officers, I'm aware of all of that. But right now, I'm really tired. And I'm ready to go home."

"Well, when you decide that you want to go ahead and file charges against this woman Frances, who allegedly assaulted you, then this will be the case number I will file my report under."

The black officer handed me his card with a number written on the back of it. I took the card, thanked them for their time and walked off towards my car.

Now from the angle I was walking, I could see both officers as they watched me get into my car. And I could also tell that they were saying something about my car because as I began to drive out of the parking lot, the white officer started writing something down onto his note pad. But I didn't care, 'cause I kept right on riding. I figured if they ever wanted to catch up to me, all they had to do was run the tags from my car and stop by my crib later.

Still hyped up from everything that just went down, I wanted nothing else but to vent my frustrations, so I pulled out my cell phone and called my cousin Nikki.

"Where you at?" I asked her the second she answered her cell phone.

"Just getting in the house. Why?"

"Girl, you won't believe what just happened to me a few minutes ago."

"What happened?" Nikki asked me in an urgent manner.

"I almost went to jail."

"How?"

"For trying to beat the brakes off Ricky's baby mama, Frances."

"Where?"

"In the parking lot of the Taco Bell off Independence and Virginia Beach Boulevard."

"Wait! Now, you've got to be kidding me."

"No, I'm not."

"Tell me what happened?"

"Well, I had just walked into the joint and noticed Frances with some ol' cornball ass nigga, leaving the front of the line because they had just got their food. And then they started walking in the direction I was standing. So, when she saw me, she walked over to me and called me a snitch, saying one of her girlfriends named Freda saw me coming from out of the FBI building right before Ricky got picked up by the Feds. So I told her to get outta my face with that bullshit because her girlfriend don't know what the hell she's talking about."

"Now, how did her girlfriend see all that?"

"She said her friend cleans up the building right across the street from the FBI building."

"Oh, shit! That's not good."

"Who the fuck you telling," I commented in agitation.

"So, what else did she say?"

"Nothing, but that she was gon' tell Ricky when he call her again."

"Well, what did you do when she told you that?"

"I just told her she was crazy and walked away from her. But this hoe got real bold and started walking behind me. So when we got outside, I cussed her out and talked about her daughter and that's when this bitch sucker punched me in my face."

"What!? You're lying!"

"No, I'm not, girl. And once I had realized this trick hit me, I stole her ass right dead in her face. And trust me, I went for blood 'cause her face was bleeding real bad after I buried my wedding ring in her skin."

"So, what was she doing?"

"Nikki, she wasn't doing nothing but talking shit! Because I couldn't feel none of them soft-ass punches she was throwing at me."

"Well, where was the guy she was with when all of this was going on?"

"He was in his car. But when he saw me standing over top of her and beating her ass, he decides that he wants to come to her rescue."

"Well, what did he do?"

"He grabbed one of my arms and told me to get off of her. So I told him to get the fuck off of me. And while me and him was going back and forth, Frances reached up and grabbed a big hunk of my hair and started twisting it into a knot. So, I'm real mad now because I got a nigga who I don't even know, holding my arm while some hoe I cannot stand got me bent over with a chunk of my hair wrapped up in the palm of her hand."

"Girl, I sure wish I was there because that shit would not have went down like that."

"I know. But it's all good, 'cause that hoe is gon' see me again. And when she do, I'm gon' bury her and her daughter's stinking asses."

Nikki laughed at my comment and then asked, "So, who broke y'all fight up?"

"It was nobody really. Because after somebody from the crowd yelled out and said, that the police was coming, I got up from off her. And that's when her and her boyfriend jumped in his car and drove off."

"Well, do you think she's going to tell Ricky what her friend Freda told her?"

"Hell yeah! I mean, especially after what happened today."

"So, what are you going to do?"

"I don't know."

"Well, what do you think he gon' say when she tells him?"

"I don't know."

"Well, we're gonna have to figure something out. Because I know him well enough to know that when he finds out what really went down, he's gon' wanna have something done to us."

"Don't worry 'bout that because that ain't gon' happen."

"Well, since you know your husband better than I do, I'm going to let you run the show."

"Yeah, let me do that," I told Nikki and then I got quiet for a second because I was trying to collect my thoughts.

"Hey," Nikki said to me, "You all right?"

"Yeah. I'm a'ight."

"Well, act like it. 'Cause you're scaring the hell outta me."

"Oh, shut up! Wit'cha dramatic ass!"

We both laughed but deep down inside, I knew she was somewhat scared because I was beginning to feel the same way. But, I ain't gon' panic. Everything will work out.

AFTER MAIL CALL

At mail today, the C.O. gave me a kite from Sunshine. I went on back into my cell and climbed onto my bunk for some privacy. In the kite, she started saying how much she loves me. And that she missed the times when we was on the streets. And how we use to take weekend trips and fuck the whole time. The letter also said that her lawyer found a couple of loopholes in her case, so they filed for an appeal to get her sentence over-turned, which looked real good. And that if she's granted immediate release, then she's gon' get out and start working on getting my case back in court, too.

Now I ain't gon' front, 'cause all that shit she's talking sounds real sweet to a player-ass nigga like me. But I know that as soon as that hoe hits the free world, everything gon' change real quick. So my best bet is to try and get Kira back on my team. She's the only woman in my life who'll make sure shit is straight with me. But now, since she done found out about me and Sunshine, I know it's gon' be real hard trying to re-recruit her and get her back on the grind. I just hope that she don't take too long to come to her senses, 'cause right now, the clock is ticking. And I sho' would hate to sic my street soldiers on her. But that's just how shit rolls with me. I mean, you're either with me or you're against me. And that's just how the game is played. Now, don't get me wrong, because I love the fuck outta my wife, Kira, even though I got a shitty way of showing it. And I know I could've done shit a lot different, but that's just how I'm built. I ain't no Romeo type of cat. I'ma gangsta-ass nigga. I'm raw and a killer at will. So, the way I showed my love is by making sho' she had everything she wanted, plus some. That's why she was living at the castle, driving a $40,000 whip, with a slew of fucking minks and fur coats hanging in her closet, plus a nice-ass diamond collection. And then on top of that, I kept her in the Saks and Bloomies gear.

I mean, it wasn't nothing for her to cop four or five pairs of shoes by Jimmy Choo, with the bags to match. And that's because she's Wifey. But she said that wasn't enough, which is why I always got static when I wanted to go out to the strip club or bounce out of town with a couple of my squad members. Kira knew what time it was. And trust me, I paid for it. Because it seemed like every time she found a new phone number stashed away in my car, or found out I had some new chick pregnant, my stash kept getting smaller and smaller. She thought I was stupid, but I knew what time it was too. And she found out later that I knew she knew it. So, it's all good. Now, all I'm focusing on is trying to find a way to get outta this joint. Watching all these clown-ass niggas in here makes me feel like I'm in a fucking circus. Especially when I hear them beasting about all the shit they had when they was on the bricks, when I know they ain't had shit.

Most of them crab-ass niggas was either a *hot boy*, or a *watch-out*. I mean, come on dawg! Who the fuck wants to keep hearing that bullshit over and over again? Because it damn sho' ain't me. So, if this shit don't stop soon, I'm gon' have to make an example outta one of these bitch-ass niggas in here. And it might be real soon.

"Yo, Rick," my cellmate walked up to me and said, "If you going to the chow hall, you better come on now dawg, 'cause niggas is lining up at the gate."

"Nah, Bossman, I'm straight. I'ma chill out here and eat a Cup-a-Soup or something."

"A'ight, baby boy," Bossman replied and then I watched him as he walked outta our cell.

Now, me and him done been cellmates from the day I was put in here. So, he's the only cat I fucks with . His real name is Leonard Marshall from P-Town, Portsmouth, VA. This nigga used to be the top man in the Brick City Crew. Yeah, them cats use to get plenty of paper, pumping out the greenery.

I heard they had shit going strong for six years until one of his squad members got real careless and sold ten pounds of Silver Haze to an undercover narco. And then when homeboy got cornered in that steel room by himself with them crackers, he cried like a fucking baby which is how shit went up in smoke for them. So, everybody who dealt with that clown directly fell down in the line of fire. And even though Bossman was at the top of the chopping block, he got off easy with a five year sentence. He'll be out of this joint in four since it's state time. His homeboy got off with only two pies.

Lucky for him. I just wish I was serving a small-ass bid like that. Having the judge throw a life sentence at me without parole just ain't sitting right with me. So, something's got to give. I refuse to sit up in here for the rest of my life. It's just not going to happen. Not while I'm alive and breathing.

"Last call for chow, if anybody else is going," an old, white female C.O. yelled out loud, so that the whole block could hear her. But nobody said nothing because the block was empty, except for me. So, when she said, "All right, I guess this is it," and started locking up the gate, I jumped up from my bunk and said, "Hey C.O., you think you can take me to medical?"

"I'm sorry, but I can't do that," she told me.

"Why?" I wanted to know.

"Because I don't work on this floor. I'm just filling in until C.O. Bivens comes back from her lunch break. But I'll let C.O. Hopkins know, since he's still on the floor."

"A'ight," I said, and she walked off.

THREE DAYS LATER

After three fucking days, these slow-ass muthafuckas finally pulled me out of the block so I could go to medical. The two C.O.'s who was escorting me to the clinic was Mr. Hopkins and Ms. Bivens. Mr. Hopkins was a old, hard nose- assed nigga, who thought he could whip every nigga's ass in this joint, 'cause he used to be a Navy Seal. And since he done been working here for over fifteen years, he tried to throw his weight around a lil' bit. But I'm here to tell you that homeboy seriously don't want none of me. Because I'll bring it to him real hard. And trust me, he ain't gon' be ready.

Now I would love to give Ms. Bivens something with her fine ass. Shorty got to be every bit of twenty-five because her skin is flawless. And she looks like she's Spanish or something, 'cause she's pretty as a muthafucka. And that ass she got is beautiful. It's round, plump and ripe like I love it. Even though them uniform pants ain't giving her no justice. But, guess what? I got eyes like Superman, so I can see it. And not only that, I would give this chick every dime I got on canteen just to see it in the flesh. Oh, but don't get me wrong, 'cause I'll fuck her, too, bad as I want some pussy. A nigga like me is tired of beating his shit in the shower. Shit, I want to run up in some wet pussy real bad. And if Shorty right here wants the job, then she can get hired on the spot.

Now, as soon as I walked in the clinic, Hopkins had Bivens cuff me to the chair because he had to leave and go get another inmate. I guess he figured she'll be all right alone with me because there was another C.O. in the next room with the doctor.

So I sat back in the chair and leaned my head up against the wall. I mean, even though I was in jail, it felt real good to be out of that little-ass cell block. And I'm thinking that my face must've shown it, because the minute I closed my eyes C.O. Bivens said, "What are you here to see the doctor for? Because if you ask me, you don't look sick at all."

Now before I answered her, I opened my eyes and gave her one of the most handsomest smiles I could give and said, "It may not look like it, but my throat is sore as hell. And plus, I got a bad headache."

"You aren't lying to me now, are you?" she asked as she cracked a smile.

"Nah, Ma. I ain't lying to you."

"My name is Bivens, not Ma."

"Oh, damn! My bad," I apologized, hoping that it'll get her to open up a little bit more to me. And guess what? It worked. Because the next thing she said was, "Can I ask you a question?"

"Yeah, go 'head."

"How come you don't get any visits?"

"What, you got me under a microscope?"

She giggled a little bit and then she replied, "Call it what you want. But remember, I work here, so I know everything."

"Yeah, except for why I don't get no visits."

She smiled at me again and said, "But I will if you tell me."

Gosh Almighty! I can't believe I got Shorty talking her ass off to me. Plus, I'm getting her to smile every time I make a comment. Now, how sweet is that? But, it can get even sweeter if she would let me take her phat ass in one of these closets so I can fuck the hell out of her. Boy, I can picture it now, having that red, juicy ass bent over, playing tug-a-war with her pussy wrapped around my dick. She wouldn't know what hit her after I'm done tagging her.

Oh and she can get it in the butt hole, too. It don't matter to me, just as long as I get my nut off. But anyway, I went on and answered her question by saying, "The reason why I don't get no visits is because I don't have anybody on the outside I want to see."

"But aren't you married?"

"Yeah."

"So, why don't you want to see your wife?"

"Because we ain't together no more."

"But you're still married, though."

"I know. But right now we're separated."

"Do y'all have kids together?"

"Nope. We sho' don't."

"Well, I know it's got to be hard on you," she commented like she was concerned.

"Nope. Not really. I mean, you can't miss nothin' you ain't really have."

"So, how are you dealing with the time they gave you?"

"I just don't think about it. But I got my lawyer working on my appeal though," I lied.

"Well, that's good. I wish you the best of luck."

"I don't need luck. I just need to keep feeding my lawyer his dough so he can do what he do best. And a good woman to stay on top of him," I replied, trying to give her a hint.

"Well, finding a good woman shouldn't be that hard. All you have to do is have one of your cell buddies back there to hook you up with a pen-pal."

"Nah. I ain't trying to find a woman that way. Keeping them cats back in the block out of my business is top priority for me."

"Well, how can that be when almost everybody in the jail knows who you are?"

"Yeah, they think they know who I am because the Feds said that I was the head nigga in my organization and that I supplied damn near the whole East coast with coke. And that I generated over fifty million dollars in an eight year period. But, I'm here to tell you that most of that shit is a lie."

"Well, what about the murders?"

"What about 'em?"

"Did you really order those people to be killed?"

"Hell nah!" I replied, lying my ass off. And then I sucked my teeth like I couldn't believe she asked me that shit. "My right hand man ordered that hit."

"Did you know about it?"

"Damn! You sho' asking a lot of questions like you the police or something. But nah, I ain't know about it until after it happened."

"Oh, I'm sorry!" she said all apologetic and shit!

But I realized she ain't doing nothin' but acting like a typical woman. Wanna know every damn thing. So I smiled at her and said, "You a'ight! But now since you know all my business you got to tell me if you got a man or not?"

"I can't tell you anything about my personal life," she replied in a sassy, but hard-to-get type of way. But I knew deep down inside she wanna tell me for-real. So, I came back on her and said, "Well, that's cool. But, just know this..."

"What?" she asked trying real hard not to crack a smile.

"That if you need anything don't ever hesitate to tell me."

"And what could you possibly do for me?" she asked me sounding eager like a muthafucka'.

I laid my pimp shit down and told her, "For one, I can pay all your bills. I can keep you in one of them all-day spas every week. And if you act right, I could replace that little joint on your finger with something *icier*."

"Now, what's wrong with my ring?" she asked me like I had just embarrassed her.

I told her, "Ain't nothin' wrong with it. I just feel like you deserve to be wearing something bigger. I mean, 'cause first of all, if you was my biddy, you wouldn't be working here around all these niggas. It's too dangerous. And not only that, I know these crackers ain't paying you no more than $11 to $12 an hour. And that's pennies."

"I make more than that," she spoke up and said it like she was getting on the defensive, which is why I know she's lying. But, I'ma let her ride that pipe dream if she wants to.

So anyway, right before I was getting ready to throw another piece of bait at her, the fucking doctor brought his gay-looking ass from out of his office and asked Bivens to escort me in there. So right when she leaned over to uncuff me from the chair, I whispered to her and asked her was she gon' think about what I said? And that's when she told me that she'll think about it, which is all good, because whether she knows it or not, she just took that bait off my hook. So, it ain't gon' be too much longer before I'll be able to pull that ass in. And trust me, I'ma handle it when I do.

Now my visit with that fake-ass doctor only took about five minutes and then he booted my ass right on out of there with a cup of salt water and two fucking Tylenols.

But what's so crazy about it is that the muthafucka' charged me ten dollars for it. Now, that's straight gangsta for a nigga's ass.

As soon as I got back in the cellblock, I got a hold to one of the phones, 'cause I needed to make some connections on the outside. I called my baby mama Frances first because she got three-way and plus I wanted to see if she was home so I could talk to my *likkle pickney.* After I sat back and waited for a few, I heard Frances pick up the phone and say hello. I got happy as hell. I mean, because it's been about a month and a half since I got a phone call through to this chick. Her trifling ass ain't never home. I be wondering where my daughter be sometimes, 'cause I know she ain't always with her mama.

"Hello," she said like she was anxious.

"Yo, Frances! What's good?" I asked her.

"Ricky, I'm so glad you called me," she commented.

"Wass up?"

"I just want to let you know that I had to beat your wife's ass a couple of days ago."

"Who? Kira?"

"Yeah. That bitch!"

"What happened?"

"Well, you know I ain't seen her nothing but one time since you been locked up. So right before I ran into her day before yesterday, I saw one of my home girl's named Freda at the club about two weeks ago, and she told me that she seen Kira walking out of the FBI building not too long before they picked you up."

"How did she know it was Kira?" That's what I wanted to know because hearing Frances tell me that my wife got caught by one of her friends coming out of the Fed building ain't nothing nobody wanna assume. This is some serious shit! So I stood still and waited for her to answer me, while my heart did a ball fifty.

"Ricky," she started off saying, "Freda, knows how Kira looks. And plus, she even described her to me."

"Nah, man. That can't be," was all I could say, because my heart wouldn't let me believe that Kira would go down to the FBI building without telling me.

"Well, believe it because it true. And don't get mad when I say I told you so."

"Told me what?" I snapped because I was getting frustrated with the thought of Kira going behind my back, talking to them crackers.

"That your bitch wasn't shit! That's what!"

"Tell me where you beat her ass?" I skipped straight to the point.

"When I saw her at the Taco Bell out Virginia Beach a couple days ago."

"What happened?"

"Well, right after the people gave me my food, I turned around to leave and that's when I saw her standing at the door. So I walked up to her and she gon' have the nerve to speak to me. And that's when I said, 'Don't speak to me you fucking snitch!' So she tried to get all loud with me, talking about I better get out of her face or she gon' whip my ass. But when I got in her face more, she gon' tell me that she ain't got time for me and walked out the place. So, I walked right behind her and told her that I was going to tell you what she did."

"And what did she say?"

"You know she tried to deny it. But I told her that she was

a fucking liar because Freda works right across the street from the FBI Building, and she saw her. So after I told her that, she got loud with me again, talking about she's tired of my mouth and the reason why she didn't kick my ass a long time ago was because you told her not to."

"That's a lie. I didn't tell her no shit like that!"

"Well, that's what she said. And then she kept running her mouth about how she ain't never like Fredrica. Talking about how fucking grown she was, and that the only reason why she bothered to look after her sometimes was done on the strength of you."

"Oh, so that's what she said, huh?" I asked in a calm way. But I was mad as a muthafucka.

"Yep. She sho' did. That's why I eased up on her and *stung* her ass real good. And then she gon' come back on me with a lame ass punch. So when she saw that it didn't do anything to me, she grabbed me and got me down on somebody's car. And that's when I went off on her ass. I was fucking her up. And all she could do was hold me down, with her weak ass."

"Who broke the fight up?"

"My friend did when somebody said that the police was coming."

"And what did Kira do?"

"I don't know what she did, 'cause I hauled ass. I got a warrant."

"For what this time?"

"Failure to appear."

"On what?"

"On a boosting charge I got right after you got locked up."

"Girl, you need to chill out."

"I'm chilling. So you ain't got to worry about me."

"I'm worried about my daughter."

"Oh, she a'ight."

"Where is she anyway?"

"At my mama's house."

"Damn, man. I wanted to talk to her."

"Well, she'll be back later on this evening."

"A'ight. Well, do me a favor?"

"Wass up?"

"You still got three-way, right?"

"Yeah."

"Well, call Kira's shop for me. And if she don't answer the phone, ask for her. But act like you're trying to make a hair appointment. And when she gets on the phone, don't say nothing. Just be quiet and let me talk."

"A'ight," Frances said and then she sucked her teeth like she wasn't too happy about what I had just told her to do. But she let it go and did it anyway.

THE JUMP OFF

"Millennium Styles," I heard some chick say when she answered the phone. And since Frances knew it wasn't Kira, she asked to speak to her. The chick told her to hold on and that's when I heard her yell Kira's name, telling her she had some lady on the phone that wants to talk to her. Now, it took Kira 'bout five minutes to get her ass on the phone, but she made it before my twenty-five minute call was up.

"This is Kira," she said like she was all happy and shit. But I rained on her muthafucking parade real quick.

"What's good, Wifey?"

"Who is this?" she asked sounding all stupid, stuttering and shit. So, I played right along with her and said, "It's your darling sweet husband."

"Whatchu' want?" Her tone changed like she had a bad taste in her mouth.

"Well for starters, I wanna know why you keep sending my letters back to the jail?"

"Because I don't have time for your lies. That's why."

"Look, never mind that. I need you to come down to the

jail, so we can talk."

"About what?"

"Well, because I'm gon' need you to get in touch with Papi."

"For what?"

"Because I need to get a job done."

"Well, I'm telling you right now that I'm not about to get into none of that shit you and Papi got going on."

"Nah, Kira. It ain't even like that. That's why I need you to come down here, so I can tell you what's going on."

"Why you can't tell me now?"

"Because I got a whole bunch of niggas looking in my muthafucking mouth."

"Well, I don't know what to tell you."

"Come on now, Kira, this shit is important."

"Okay, and I believe you. But I am not coming down to that jail."

"Oh, so it's like that?"

"Yes. It's just like that. So, don't act like you don't know what time it is."

"Look Kira, I didn't call to argue with you."

"Well, good. Because I've got clients waiting on me."

"Okay. But can you hold up a minute?"

"What is it, Ricky?"

"Tell me what happen between you and Frances?"

"Why you want to hear it from me? I mean, I know she done already told you what happened."

"Yeah. She told me. So I just wanna know, is it true that you went down to the FBI building to talk to them crackers like right before they picked me up?"

"Hell nah! That shit ain't true! You know I wouldn't do no grimy shit like that."

"Okay. But why is that chick Freda saying that she saw you?"

"Look, that's something you need to ask her."

"Nah. But I'm asking you."

"And I'm the wrong person to answer that question."

"So, what are you saying?" I asked her because she was beginning to piss me the fuck off.

"Ricky, all I'm going to say about that is you're going to believe what you wanna believe. But I ain't been down to no FBI Building. So your informant got me mixed up with somebody else."

"Well, it doesn't matter."

"Whatchu mean it doesn't matter?"

"Well, because I'm gon' get my lawyer to check it out for me."

"Oh, so you saying you don't believe me?"

"I ain't saying that..."

"Look, don't play games with me," she cut me off, "Because that's exactly what you're saying. So just know that I don't give a fuck what you do. Because you can't do shit to me. Not no more. And I mean that! All them days of you fucking around on me with dirty bitches and bringing three different kids home to me with their trifling ass baby mama's is over."

"Bitch! If anybody's trifling, it's your ass!" Frances yelled out.

"Now Ricky, I know goodness well you ain't get that skank ass hoe to call me on three-way."

"Bitch, you're the skank!"

"You know what, Ricky? Talk to your project ass baby-mama, 'cause I ain't got time for this shit!" Kira told me and then she hung up. And right before I got ready to blast Frances ass for opening up her fucking mouth, the time on my call ran out. So I called her back. And as soon as my call went through, I lit her stupid ass up.

"Now why the fuck did you open your fucking mouth? Didn't

I tell you to be quiet?"

"Yeah. But she started talking shit about me."

"Who the fuck cares! I had some real important shit to tell her. So all you had to do was just be quiet until after I said what I had to say. I mean, come on, dawg! I'm in a real fucked-up situation right now, and only her dumb ass can help me get out of it. So the next time you hear that bitch say something about you while you got me on your three-way, don't say nothing. Just go on up to the shop and beat her ass again. That's all."

"But...," she started to explain but I cut her off and said, "But nothing, Frances. Don't do that shit again. A'ight?"

She sucked her teeth and said, "A'ight."

After that was settled, I flipped the script on her ass and acted like nothing happened. "Whatcha wearing?" I started off saying.

"Whatcha mean?" she asked me.

"I mean, whatcha got on?"

"Oh, nothing but a light blue tube top and a blue and white tennis skirt."

"What kind of panties you wearing?"

"Come on, Ricky. You know I don't wear nothing but thongs."

"Damn! I bet that ass still look phat to death."

"You know it," she commented in a bragging way.

"Won'tcha come on down here, so I can see it."

"Now you know I ain't trying to run into Kira."

"That bitch ain't coming down here!"

"Well, when are your visiting days?"

"We got 'em today and Saturday."

"What time?"

"From eleven to nine."

"A'ight, then. I'ma come."

"What time?"

"I'll be down there by seven."

"Good. 'Cause I wanna see your ass in that thong so I can beat my dick."

Frances laughed at me and said, "Ricky, them people gon' put my ass out of that visiting room if I try to pull my skirt up and show you my ass."

"They ain't gon' see it if you get the spot at the end by the wall. Shit, niggas in here get their girls to do that shit all the time."

"Well, I guess I'm gonna have to show you these titties too since you ain't seen them in a long time."

"Yeah, that sounds good," I replied.

That's the type of action I need right now since it's been a minute since I got me some pussy. So before we got disconnected, I grilled her about two more times so she wouldn't forget about getting that spot. I told her that if somebody else beat her to it, then she might as well carry her ass home 'cause I ain't gon' be in the mood to talk. I wanna see some ass. And that's it!

A FEW MINUTES LATER

"That was Ricky, wasn't it?" Rhonda asked me right after following me out the back door of the shop.

"Yep," I said, as if I was utterly disgusted.

"So, what did he say?" she asked. And since I didn't feel like going through the whole spill about the shit with me supposedly snitching on Ricky, I told her, "Nothing. But he wants me to come down to the jail to see him."

"Well, what did he say to you to make you cuss him out like you did?"

"Girl, that muthafucka' had a nerve to flip out on me like I'm suppose to be down for him or something."

"Now, I know you lying!" Rhonda exclaimed.

"No, I'm not. That's why I flipped out on his stupid ass! And told him don't call me, call them trifling-ass baby mamas of his. And just so happens his baby-mama Frances was on the other end and heard me. So, she said, *"Bitch, you the one trifling!"* So, I got right back in her ass real quick. And then I jumped in his and told them both to kiss my ass and hung up."

"That's what his ass gets. Got that hoe on the other end listening to y'all conversation like that shit is cool."

"I know," I said and then I sighed. "He always does some of the stupidest shit known to man."

"Did y'all bring up the subject about Sunshine?"

"Hell nah! I mean for what? She sho' ain't no threat to me, sitting behind bars with his dumb ass. That's exactly what they asses get. They deserve one another."

"You sho' ain't lying about that. I just can't believe how she had the balls to come in this shop everyday doing hair at her station and smiling like she was your friend and then as soon as she steps foot out the front door, she's dead on your husband's dick. Now tell me that ain't some scandalous shit!"

"Yeah, it was. And that's why their both paying for it now, with their nasty asses!"

"Did you tell him that you're filing for divorce?"

"Nah, I ain't tell him. I'm just going to wait until he gets the papers."

"So, how long is that going to take?"

"Well, my lawyer told me that we're going to have to be separated for a year before a judge will grant it."

"But, did you tell your lawyer that Ricky is locked up?"

"Yeah, but he said that it didn't matter," I began telling her. Before I could finish my sentence, the back door to the shop opened and out came my cousin, Nikki.

"There you are," she said, smiling from ear to ear.

So I smiled back and replied, "What's up with that big-ass smile on your face?"

"Yeah. Who done made you all happy and shit?" Rhonda interjected.

"I just met this guy named Syncere from New Jersey. And believe me when I tell you, that that cat is fine to death."

"Girl, don't be falling for niggas from up top. 'Cause they'll get your ass in trouble."

"Nikki, don't listen to cousin's male-bashing ass because he might be a winner. Now tell me what kind of whip he's driving."

"A silver Range Rover."

"What year?" Rhonda's questions continued.

"I don't know but it looks like a 2005 model."

"Did he tell you what he does for a living?" I asked her because so far it sounds like this cat Syncere is a fucking hustler.

"Well, he said he owns that car wash off Brambleton Ave. It's right across the street from Norfolk State University."

"That ain't nothing but a front," I commented.

Rhonda sucked her teeth and responded, "You don't know that for sure."

"Yeah, you're right. But these days you can't believe everything a nigga tells you."

"Now, I'll agree with you on that," Rhonda interjected once more. And again, before I could get a word in, the back door to the shop opened up. This time it was April poking her head outside the door. "Rhonda, Tony told me to tell you to come out front."

"What? He was beeping the horn or something?" Rhonda asked.

"Nah. He called the phone and told me to tell you to come outside. So, I told him okay."

"A'ight. Thanks," Rhonda told April as she began to put herself in motion to walk back into the salon. "I'll be right back y'all," she told me and Nikki and then she was off.

Now after the back door closed and Rhonda was out of sight, I took a deep breath and told Nikki that I had something very important to tell her.

"What is it?" she wondered aloud.

I immediately pulled her a couple of feet away from the building and said, "Frances told Ricky what happened."

"Well, what exactly did she tell him?"

"Everything."

"And how do you know?"

"Because I just got off the phone with him."

"So, what did he have to say?"

"Well, he wanted to know why was me and Frances fighting? And then he asked me was it true that Frances friend saw me coming out of the FBI building?"

"And what did you say?" Nikki asked me as I noticed how big her eyes were protruding.

"Whatcha mean, *'what I said?'* Shit! I ain't crazy! You know I denied it. But I know he didn't believe me because he asked me why would that chick lie on me? I told him I didn't know. And that's when he said he was going to get his lawyer to check it out. So you know when he said that I was about to shit bricks! But instead of cracking up, I reversed the game on him and told him to do what the fuck he felt was necessary because he should know that I wouldn't do nothing sheisty like that. And when I said it, I was snapping. So I'm hoping that I was dramatic enough and he believed me."

"But what if he didn't?"

"Then me and you are going to have to put our heads together."

"And do what?" Nikki asked me in an agitated manner.

This was an instant reminder of how terrified she gets when forced into a corner. And the fact that I know she's getting really worried about what we were about to be up against if Ricky found out the truth. And the last thing I want to do is have her walking 'round here acting all paranoid and shit. That's why I came back on her and said, "Look, everything's going to be all right because he's not going to call his lawyer. And even if he did, he still wouldn't be able to do shit. I mean, look where he's at. On fucking lockdown! So, stop fretting."

"Easy for you to say. Remember, he doesn't give a fuck about me."

"Well, if this will make you feel any better, just know that your name never came up in our conversation."

"Oh, but sooner or later it will. Especially if his lawyer finds out what really went down in those FBI files."

"But, he won't. I promise you."

Nikki sighed heavily and replied, "I just hope you're right." And then she left me standing where I was to go back into the shop.

Now I ain't gonna lie, I wished I could've told Nikki more convincing shit than that, but I just couldn't come up with the right stuff to say. So, maybe it's best that it came out the way that it did. I mean, she definitely needs to know what position to play because whether she wants to know it or not, the game done already started. So in the end, somebody will win. I just hope that it's going to be us.

DIGGING UP OL' FEELINGS

This baby is really starting to get to me. I mean, it ain't that bad, considering I don't get the early morning sickness everyday. But I am always getting that never-ending nauseating feeling. That's why I decided to take today off, so I can lounge at home. But then, that got old. And that's why I'm riding around in my car, looking for a detailing spot, so I can get my car washed. And then it dawned on me to take a trip down to that spot in Norfolk on Brambleton Avenue, owned by the cat Nikki was bragging about. This way, when I see him, I can draw my own conclusions about his slick ass. Shit, he is not going to have my cousin's nose all wide open. It just ain't going to happen, if I can help it.

Now moments after I arrived this old-looking dude, who was probably a crackhead, walked up to my car and asked me to pull it behind this candy-apple red Suburban sitting on huge–assed, chromed-out rims. So I did. And then I got out to cop myself a seat in one of the chairs that was put outside in front of the building for the customers to sit and watch their cars being washed and detailed. Unfortunately, all the seats were taken, so I had to just stand there. But luckily, there was a gentleman in this circle who saw that I desperately needed a seat. Then again, it could've been this Michael Kors baby-doll dress I'm rocking because my body is making this thing look really tasty on me.

"Here you go, Shorty. Take my seat," he insisted.

I smiled at him and told him thanks. And then right after I sat down, I noticed this tall, light-skinned chick from the corner of my eye, who was sitting like three chairs over to my right, *gritting* at me. I turned around to face her and gave her a nasty look like, *Do you know me or something?* But, I guess she couldn't read between the lines because this hoe started gritting on me even harder.

I asked her, "Do you know me from somewhere?"

And this hoe got straight hood with me and said, "If I did, I would've spoken to you by now!"

I laughed at her smart-ass comment and replied, "Well then why are you staring at me?"

"Excuse me, honey, but I am not staring at you. I'm looking past you if you must know."

"Could've fooled me," I replied sarcastically. I didn't say it loudly. I remained a lady and said it in a calm manner. But it was loud enough for her red ass to hear me. I just couldn't let her punk me down in front of all these niggas out here. I'm too fly for that type of shit. And even though I'm far from being scared to get at her ass, I wasn't dressed appropriately for the occasion. Right now, I am in no mood to kick some hoe's ass in this seven hundred-dollar dress. It's just not going to happen.

After I said what I had to say, I turned my body in a catty-corner position, crossed my legs and looked in the other direction. Good thing that I didn't have to sit with her for long because not even five minutes later, her little Dodge Neon was ready for her to drive off in, which was like the best thing that could've happen.

The guy who gave me his chair took her seat without question. But, he did have a question for me after we both witnessed her drive off the lot.

"Yo, Shorty, you a'ight?"

"No doubt!" I replied with confidence.

"Well for a minute there, I thought you and home girl was going to get busy."

Now before I responded to this cat's comment, I smiled at him once again, simultaneously picking what little lint balls I noticed I had on my dress and told him, "Trust me, baby. She wasn't ready for me. That's why our little chat ended quickly."

"Well, I'm glad it did. Because you're looking too good right now to be out here scrapping like cats."

"Thanks," I replied and then I giggled. I'm assuming that was an invitation for him to continue on conversing with me because he didn't hesitate to ask me if I had a man. I told him no. And that's when he asked me, "Well, who gave you that gigantic glacier on your finger?"

"Oh, this ain't nothing," I began saying, "My husband gave me this when we got married."

"But I thought you just said you didn't have a man?"

"I don't. Me and my husband aren't together anymore."

"So, what, y'all divorced?"

"We're in the process of making that happen."

"Damn! I know homeboy ain't too happy 'bout that."

"Well, to be honest, I don't know how he's feeling because we ain't been together for almost three months now. And we don't talk."

"So, what do you do when you're all alone?"

"I read a lot of books. And when I get sick of that, I'll take myself shopping."

"Where you like shopping at?"

"Wait a minute! You sho' asking me a whole lot of questions and I don't even know your name." I made a casual observation.

He raised his eyebrows like he was caught off guard and said, "Damn, I'm sorry. My name is Tyree."

"Hi, Tyree. I'm Kira," I told him as I extended my hand to shake his.

"Damn! Your hand is soft as hell."

"Thanks," I replied and then I pulled my hand back out of his.

"Do you think I'll be able to take you out?" he wanted to know. But before I answered his question, I took one long look at him from head to toe. Yeah, he seems like a cool cat to hang out with. But I wasn't at all digging his height. I mean, he has to be every bit of 5'2", which is three inches shorter than I am. So, I'm dissatisfied with that part from the door. However, he is making shit happen with his attire. I'm loving the hell out of his tan-linen shirt, with the shorts to match. And that huge-ass *iceberg* dangling from that platinum link around his neck got to be worth more than $50k. And since I know my jewelry, there's no question in my mind that this nigga is stacking major chips. And when there's plenty of chips involved, hoes will follow. So, I think I'll pass on this one.

"Nah, baby," I began to say. "I don't think that will be a good idea."

"But why?"

"Because, I'm not ready."

"Is there anyway that I can change your mind?" he wanted to know.

"Nope," I assured him. So, he stood up from his chair because one of the carwash guys walked up to him and handed him his keys.

"Y'all finished?" he asked the attendant.

"Yeah. Your car is right over there," the guy told him and that's when Tyree pulled out a huge knot of dough from his pockets and hit the guy off with a fifty spot.

"Keep the change," Tyree told him. And then he looked back at me and said, "I hope I see you again."

"You just might. If you keep your eyes open."

"Oh, I will. Because that's a must in my profession," he replied and then he walked off.

He hopped in a Chrysler 300-Hemi sitting on twenty-twos, cranked up the loud sounds of Kanye West's joint "Golddigger," and drove out of the parking lot, squealing his tires like he's a fucking stunt driver or something. I guess he did it because he thought it was gangsta. Boy, does he have a lot to learn.

Now, I didn't have to wait much longer for my car, which was right up my alley. After I paid the guy who handed me my keys, I headed on over to my car to inspect it. And while I was doing that, Nikki's newfound friend and Mr. Car Wash owner pulls up in his silver Range Rover HSE. So you know that I was not about to leave until I saw this cat for myself. He is the main reason why I came all this way.

I continued to stand over by my car like I was still giving it a full inspection. And then finally the driver side door opens and out comes this six foot tall, fine-ass nigga. But, what threw me for a loop was that it wasn't Nikki's friend Syncere who had just stepped out of the truck—it was my old flame, Quincy.

And without giving it a second thought, I rushed right on over there to him.

"Q," I yelled.

He turned around and the moment I was within arms reach of him, I said, "Boy, whatcha doing up here?"

"Hey baby," he spoke to me and then he embraced me.

"You can let me go now," I said sarcastically, which made him laugh. But he did release me from his arms.

And once he did that, he said, "Whatcha doing in this part of town?"

"I just got my car detailed. But you ain't answered my question," I told him.

"Oh, I got my joint cleaned too."

"So, you pushing a Range now, huh?"

"Nah. This is my man's joint. I just borrowed it to make a quick run. My whip is over there," he replied as he pointed to the same 7-series BMW, I saw him driving a few months back when he was with his chick from D.C., who looked like she attended Howard University.

"So, where is he?" My questions kept coming.

"He's probably in the office."

"Where? In there?" I asked him, probing for more information as I pointed towards the small building on the lot, even though I already knew the answer.

"Yeah. Me and him just took over this joint about a month ago because the last owner was in a bunch of fucking debt. He hooked up with Syncere and then Syncere called me to go in with him 'cause he needed some extra *ends*. I told him let's do this. And here we are."

"So, how's business?"

"Business is good. I mean, we be coming off with at least a grand a day."

"Word?"

"Hell yeah! 'Cause when niggas bring their whips through here, they be wanting wax jobs and the gloss treatments for their rims, which is forty bones alone. So you do the math and multiply that number by thirty."

"Damn, Quincy. Y'all pulling in some cheese."

"I know. That's why I be trying to figure out how that other dude got in so much debt. 'Cause money comes through this spot on a regular."

"Well, it must be real nice," I commented.

"Yeah. It's cool. Because it got my parole officer off my ass."

"Oh, so your P.O. knows you're part owner of this place?"

"Hell nah! He thinks I'm one of the workers."

"Quincy, you always got some shit going on," I said and then smiled.

"Yeah. But I ain't the only one," he began saying. "I heard you and Ricky had plenty shit on y'all plates, too."

"Ricky does. But I don't."

"Damn. That's fucked up!"

"Yep. It sho' is. But what's really fucked up is when you try so hard to be down for your man and he takes you for granted. That's why I've decided that it's time to start looking out for myself."

"What? Y'all ain't together no more?"

"Nope. I'm filing for a divorce."

"So, how much time did he get? 'Cause I heard some niggas back in D.C. said the Feds gave him thirty. And then I heard somebody else say he got life."

"Well, it damn sho' wasn't thirty."

"Goddamn! Now I know that nigga got to be sick about that shit! I mean, he ain't gon' ever see the streets again. And that's some real shit to deal with ."

"Well, he made his bed. Now he's going to have to lay in it."

"But how can you say that, Kira? I mean, it's not like that nigga got like a five-to-ten-year bid. He's got to live in the pen for the rest of his life. He ain't gon' ever be able to come home."

"What? You think I don't know that?" I replied sarcastically.

"You sho' don't act like it," he began saying. "I'm just so glad that I am not in ol' boy's shoes. 'Cause I'll probably be trying to get somebody to do something to your ass for gettin' ghost on me."

"Well, I guess I can count my blessings, huh, gangsta?"

"Oh, I ain't no gangsta. Your husband and his peoples are the gangstas. And speaking of gangstas, wasn't that nigga Russ down with Ricky?"

"Yeah. Why?" I asked anxiously while feeling the butterflies in my stomach.

"Because niggas back home was wondering what was up with him and why he was the only one from that crew that didn't get indicted."

"Well, I don't know nothing about that. Why you asking about Russ? You seen him or something?"

"Yeah. I see him every time I go back home. Shit, last week I saw him whipping up the block in a money-green Bentley Coupe."

"Damn! He's getting it like that?"

"Yeah. I heard that cat Papi got him on his payroll. Which is probably true 'cause the last time I saw him, he was just leaving Papi's store with his girl."

"Oh, he got a girl?" I wanted so desperately to know.

"Yeah. Him and Jessica done been together for a minute now. And they just had a baby, too."

"You sure know a whole lot of stuff about Russ."

"Baby girl, I know about every cat that lives in D.C. Especially niggas like Russ who love playing Big Dawg. You know their shit gonna be on blast."

"Well, what's your story?" I asked, trying to change the subject. Hearing about Russ and his baby-mama was making me sick to my stomach. Plus, my feelings started flipping out on me. I mean, how could that muthafucka' play me like that? Lying about having a girl after all this time. And then on top of that, got that hoe and their baby riding shot gun in a brand new fucking Bentley Coupe my money bought. But he'll get his.

I'm going to make sure of that! One way or another....

"Yo, Q," I heard a guy yell, which instantly shifted my attention to his direction. And there, peeping his head from around the glass door, was this brown-skinned and very handsome guy with a perfectly cut Caesar. I'm assuming this must be Syncere.

"What's good?" Quincy asked him.

"Yo, I got somebody on the phone that I need you to talk to."

"A'ight," Qunicy told him and then Syncere disappeared back into the building.

"So, I'm guessing that was Syncere, huh?"

"Yeah. That was him. Let me get in there so I can find out what's going on. But come back and see me sometime."

"Will you let me get my car detailed for free?"

"No question! But you gon' have to call me and let me know when you coming."

"No problem. I can do that. But you're going to have to give me your number first."

"You got something to write with ?"

"Nah. 'Cause I'ma put it in my cell phone."

After he gave me his cell phone number, I said goodbye, got in my car and left.

On my way home, I began to picture Russ in my mind, who was driving that Bentley all around D.C., playing chauffeur with his fucking family. While I'm here all alone and pregnant with his baby, pushing a two-year-old LS 400. Man, I am so angry! Ugggggg! How dare that piece of shit! Playing with my emotions like this. Oh, but his time is coming! I'ma make sure of that. And now that I think about it, if I play my cards right, I could probably get Quincy to run up on Russ. Especially if I turn around and tell him that I found out Russ is a snitch. And that he ratted out Ricky's whole crew. That's why he was able to walk away.

Boy, I can definitely see it now. Word will leak into the streets about that bastard. And since niggas don't like fucking with snitches, it's going to be just a matter of time before he's taken out of the equation. And then my life will be right back to normal again. Now, how sweet does that sound?

Immediately after I got into my apartment, I got on the phone and called Nikki. I ran everything Quincy told me down to her. But she was more interested in why I went down to Syncere's car wash. So I lied and told her that I just happened to be in the neighborhood and saw Q, and that's when he invited me over to a free wash. I'm guessing that she bought my lie, 'cause her next question was, *Did you get to see my friend, Syncere?* I told her yeah, but it was for a brief second, which wasn't enough information for her because she wanted to know what he was doing when I saw him, what he was wearing, and whether or not there were any chicks sniffing up his ass.

But before I could answer her, coincidently this nigga beeps in on her other line. So, of course, Nikki tells me to call her back. And since we didn't finish our conversation, she's going to call me as soon as she hangs up with him. I just hope she don't let him fill her head up with a lot of bullshit 'cause from the way I see it, he's got a lot of it to dish out.

ALL OR NOTHING

After I finished eating that nasty-ass garbage everybody called lunch, I went back to my cell and saw my cellmate moping 'round like he lost his girl or something. So, I sat down on the cold-ass toilet seat right next to his bed and asked him was he a'ight.

"Yeah. I'm a'ight. I was thinking 'bout some stupid-ass shit my girl just asked me on the phone a few minutes ago."

"What she say?"

"She asked me was I calling this broad I use to fuck with name Sharney, so I told her, nah. And then she started screaming on me, saying I'm lying, 'cause somebody told her a whole bunch of bullshit. So, I cut her off and told her I wasn't trying to hear that nonsense. So she got mad and hung up on me."

"Man, dontcha hate when they do dumb shit like that?"

"Hell yeah! I hate it."

"Me too, because my wife is good for that. But it's funny, 'cause, when I was on the streets, she used to be all up my ass. Always in my muthafucking pockets and spending my dough on eighteen-hundred-dollar Fendi boots, three-thousand-dollar Roberto Cavalli dresses and ten-thousand-dollar Russian sables."

"Yo, I got my girl one of them furs, too." Bossman jumped in and said.

"So, you feeling me, then," I said.

"You damn right I'm feeling you. But they ain't feeling us. Especially when they stressing us out over dumb ass shit. I mean, come on, dawg. I ain't trying to hear that. I wanna hear, 'I love you. Baby, I just sent you a letter. And I can't wait 'til you come home.' All that other shit she can keep."

"Word, dawg. I was telling my wife a couple days ago that she needs to step her game up a little, and stop worrying 'bout shit she can't change. 'Cause I'm gon' always do what I do. I made the dough. I put her ass in that three-hundred-thousand-dollar crib. Bought her a brand new LS400. Put a twelve-thousand-dollar iceberg on her finger. And I use to send her trick ass to California on shopping trips so she got hers. And that's when I got my shit off, too. I mean, come on, dawg, there's a lot of beautiful women out there. And the variety is in huge numbers. So when they run across a cat like me with major figures, them hoes wanted to get down. And I was all for it, 'cause ain't nothin' like new pussy."

"Boy, you got that right! Because, a nigga like me done had my share. And I mean, with some bad broads. I'm talking 'bout hoes with pretty faces, donkey asses and small waists," he replied and then laughed.

"Yeah. I done had my share of them, too. But where are their asses at now? 'Cause, as soon as a nigga goes on lock, every hoe who done said that they love you, scatters like roaches. And then when you get out, here they come, flocking right back at'cha like chickens."

"That's how them hoes roll. They ain't shit. And that's

why I ain't gon' be shit either."

"Word, dawg!" I told him. And then outta nowhere, C.O. Bivens yells out and tells me that my lawyer is here to see me. I got up and bounced.

Before she put me in this small-ass room I asked her, "Where you been at? I ain't seen you in 'bout a week?"

"I was on vacation."

"Where did you go?"

"I didn't go anywhere. I just sat at home and did a little spring cleaning."

"Well, see, if you were my girl, then I would've sent you to Cancun or something."

"But I'm not. So I guess I'm gonna have to stick to spending my time spring cleaning," she replied, grinning her ass off.

I came right back on her and said, "Come on, Bivens. Why you playing games?"

"I am not playing games."

"Well, did you think about what I said?"

"Yes." She was still smiling.

"So, what's up then?"

"What am I supposed to do for you in return?"

"Whatcha mean?"

"I mean, what are you planning to get out of making me your girlfriend and showering me with all those gifts you've been speaking about since the first time we talked?"

"Maybe just a lil' bit mo' of your time. Ya know, pulling me outta the block, so I can get some exercise every now and then."

"And take you where? Because there's not a lot of places in here that I can take you without being seen on the cameras. And anyway, I'm going to third shift in a couple of days."

"That's even better," I said, hoping it would convince her.

"Look, I don't know," she replied, sounding unsure. "But I'll see. Now go on in this room because your attorney is waiting on you."

"A'ight. Well, just get at me," I said and then she unlocked the door and I went in.

My lawyer was already sitting at the table with his brief-case opened when I walked up to him. I knew he was ready to give me whatever he had.

"What's good, Burgess?" I asked.

"Ready to get down to business?"

"Always."

"Well, first off, I finally got the federal agents to hand over your investigation files in exchange for your cooperation in bringing your connection with Papi Santos and his men down. So," he said and then sighed, "After looking through all of these reports, I found out that your sources were indeed correct."

"You fuckin' bullshitting!?"

"No. As a matter of fact, I'm not."

"So, Kira was ratting me out, huh?"

"Yes. But she also had some help."

"Who?" I asked, feeling my heart trying to jump out of my fucking chest.

"Her cousin, Nicole. The young lady who was initially ar-rested and charged with possession with intent."

"Yeah. Yeah. Yeah. I know who she is."

"Okay, well according to these records, she provided a substantial amount of information that started the whole in-vestigation on you and those other men in your organiza-tion."

"But how could she do that when she didn't hardly know nothin'?"

"Well, it has also been noted in these records that your wife provided a significant amount of information, too. I have a copy of a signed affidavit with her testimony right here."

"Word! Let me see that." I grabbed the piece of paper outta his hand.

Now as I began to read all the shit Kira told them crackers about me, the love I had for her in my heart started turning into hate. I mean, I'm really bugging! This hoe was sleeping in my muthafucking bed. Laughing and grinning in my face and serving my ass up to the police right under my nose. My own fucking wife! I can't believe this shit! I mean I know I done did some foul shit in our marriage, but I know I didn't deserve this. Not a fucking life sentence. Especially after all the shit me and her done been through. Kira was my partner. My dawg! My right hand. I trusted her with everything, 'cause I knew she had my back, regardless of what happened. But I see shit done changed now 'cause she told them where all my new stash houses were, who was running them, who was in charge of cooking up all the dope, and who made the pickups. She even told them about the shooting gallery me and my squad used to have, and about the cat I used to cop my machinery from, even though he's long gone now. She couldn't tell 'em how that nigga got put to rest, 'cause I ain't never tell her. So I guess I did something right.

But all and all, this whole thing is still fucked up. And I see right now that I'm gon' have to put an *"H"* on my chest and handle it 'cause it's on, now! Shit is about to change for that bitch and she don't even know it. I can't have that hoe running around on the streets like shit is lovely, because it ain't. And since I'm hurting right now, she gon' hurt too!

But before I get my soldiers suited up to do her ass in, I'm gon' get her stank ass to pitch this ball I'm trying to throw Papi's way. Since she's the only one who can make this mission possible. Now's the time to go through with the plan.

"Ayo Burgess," I said and then I slid the piece of paper back across the table.

"What's on your mind, Ricky?"

"Well, you know that in order for me to get this thing poppin' with Papi, I'm gon' need my wife to set up shop on the outside?"

"Yes, I'm aware of that."

"Okay, so I'm gon' need you to call her at her salon and tell her the deal. 'Cause, I done tried like a hundred times to get her to come down here so I can lay everything out, but she ain't *bucking*."

"So, what do you want me to say to her?"

"I just need you to call her and tell her that I'm gon' call her in about ten minutes after you do, so it would be in her best interest to accept my call."

"But, what if she gets irate with me?"

"Just tell her that I know everything and that if she don't accept my call and listen to what I gotta say, then she gon' have trouble."

"Ricky, that's coercion. I can't deliver your message in that fashion."

"Okay, well, just tell her what's going on with the investigation with Papi. And that I can get my sentence cut to almost nothing if she helps me."

"Okay. I can do that. Now, is there anything else?" Burgess asked me as he wrote his notes down on paper.

"Nah. But when you talk to her, just let her know how important this thing is."

"I will," he assured me and then started packing everything back into his briefcase.

"You gon' call her after you leave here, right?"

"Yes. As soon as I get into my car, I am going to phone her, so don't worry. I've got that part under control."

"A'ight, Burgess. Good looking out."

"No problem. But, don't forget to call my office sometime next week. That way, I can bring you up on the progress in the investigation."

"A'ight. I will," I told him.

He finished packing and left.

I had to sit there and wait for a C.O. to come and take me back to the block. But before that happened, I sat back and thought about how I was gon' come at Kira with the shit I had just found out. And then I thought it would be better to play the game her way and see how she could handle it with me on the sideline. Even though I didn't know the answer to that question, I knew I was gon' find out in a few minutes.

"Millennium Styles."

"Hello, may I speak with Kira?"

"This is she."

"Hi, this is Mark Burgess. Your husband's attorney."

"Yeah. What can I do for you?"

"Well, I have a message for you."

"What's the message?"

"Ricky's in desperate need to speak with you."

"Okay, now tell me something I don't already know."

"Listen, Kira..."

"I'm listening," she interjected.

"Your husband has a huge chance of getting his life sentence overturned by his judge. But in order to make this happen, he's going to need you to help him."

"And what does he need me to do?"

"He's going to need you to contact his old connection, Papi Santos, and try to set up a meeting with him of some sort."

"Wait a minute! Is he crazy? I'm not getting involved with that shit! That man is crazy!"

"We're all aware of that. But you're the only one who can do this. And besides, Ricky's already aware of your involvement in his case. So we both know that you're no stranger when it comes to helping the authorities."

"And so what does that mean?"

"Listen Kira, just accept your husband's phone call because he's going to be calling you in about ten minutes."

"To say what?"

"He can explain it better than I can."

"All right. So is that it?"

"Yes. That's it."

"Well, you have a nice day."

"You do the same, Kira."

TEN MINUTES LATER

I finally broke down and accepted Ricky's phone call. But while I was waiting for the operator to connect us, I locked myself in the back office of the shop so I wouldn't be bothered. I was a complete nervous wreck because of the fact that he knew how much I had helped the Feds out with their investigation against him. And for the first time, I was beginning to feel ashamed and embarrassed about the way I had betrayed him. What will I say in my defense when he confronts me with it? I mean, how am I going to justify what I did? This is some serious shit I'm about to go up against.

"Hello," Ricky finally said.

"Yeah," I replied in a nonchalant way, trying to feel what mood he was in.

"I see you got my message."

"Yeah, I got it."

"Well, before I get into what I need you to do, I just wanna let you know that I ain't even mad about what you did. A'ight?"

"Yeah. A'ight," I said. But deep down inside, my gut

feeling was telling me something totally different. I mean, why is he being so damn calm about all *this*? Is it because he needs me? Or is it because this is truly how he's feeling at the moment? But, if you ask me, something just ain't adding up here, and it will surface.

"Okay. Now that we got that out of the way," he continued, "Are you gon' help me get out of here?"

"Do I have a choice?" I asked because truth be told, I ain't feeling him or this conversation at all.

"Look Kira, don't play no fucking games with me. Now, are you gon' help me or not?"

"What do you want me to do?"

"Well, I'm gon' give you the number to Papi's store, 'cause I want you to call him on three-way. Now I'm gon' do all the talking, so just sit back and listen. Because I'm gon' set everything up. A'ight?"

"A'ight," I told him, which of course gave him the green light to continue on with what he had to say. Almost instantly after he gave me the number, I called Papi and got him on the line.

"What's good, Pop?" was Ricky's way of greeting Papi. He does this because Papi has always been like a father figure to him ever since he came on to the scene.

"Oh, my God! Ricky, is this you?" Papi asked him in his thick Hispanic accent.

"Yeah, it's me."

"Well, tell me what's going on? Because I had some of my people out trying to find out what went down out there in Virginia. But nobody ever gave me no straight answers. So, are you all right?"

Ricky sighed heavily and said, "Nah, I ain't all right. Them crackers got me tied to a murder beef. They gave me a life sentence for it."

"Ahh, Ricky! That's not good."

"I know. That's why I'm getting my lawyer to straighten things out. And to make sure it's done right, I'm gon' need some serious dough."

"How much do you need?"

"For now, I'm gon' need around $150K."

"Wow! That's a lot of money, amigo. And I would love to help you, but business here at the store hasn't been that good lately. It seems like no one has *moneda* to buy food anymore," Papi commented and then chuckled.

Now, I'm guessing he did this to bring a little humor to their conversation. Then Ricky said, "Well, I already got a little something put up. But if you can help me on the other end, I can get the rest up myself."

"Who would you get to do the shopping for you?" Papi wanted to know.

"My wife, Kira."

"Well, have her call me."

"She's on the phone with us right now. I got her to call you on three-way."

"*Hola, mi amor.*"

"How are you doing, Mr. Papi?" I said in a respectful tone.

"Well, I'm not doing too great. Seeing my son in trouble like this really upsets me."

"I'll be a'ight, Pop," Ricky interjected. "Just as long as I can get shit popping."

"Well, Kira, call me because Sosa and my nephew Miguel are back in Costa Rica, working. But, they'll be back within two weeks. So, I will prepare something really nice for the both of you when they return."

"Okay. That sounds good. But when is the last time you talked to Russ?" Ricky added.

"He came by here yesterday with his fiancée, Jessica. You

know, they just had a little girl?"

"Nah. I didn't know that she was pregnant."

"Yeah, she was. The baby is *hermosa* , so beautiful. And they made me the *padrino, the* godfather," Papi continued as his accent got thicker.

"*That's wassup*! Well, when you see him again, tell him I said to get at me. 'Cause I'm gon' need a favor from him, too."

"Okay. I'll let him know."

"Well, a'ight, Pop. I'm gon' bounce right now, so I can holler at my wife before the time on my call runs out. But I'll be getting back witcha before she comes up there to see you."

"Okay. Yeah. Call me."

"A'ight. Thanks."

"No problem. And I'll talk to you soon," Papi replied and then hung up.

Immediately after I clicked Papi's line off, Ricky wasted little or no time to say,

"Did you hear that Kira? We got less than two weeks to get shit popping! I'm gon' get Burgess to call you back so y'all can set up a day when you can go out and meet with them other people."

"What other people?"

"Stop playing stupid! You know who I'm talking 'bout."

"Oh, them," I said with no interest at all.

He continued by saying, "Oh yeah, and so you know, Papi is

always at his store in Northwest on M Street. Not the one on New Jersey Avenue. A'ight?"

"A'ight."

"Oh and I'm gon' let you know up front that them people is gon' want you to cop a brick or two. And they gon' probably want you to wear a wire, too."

"A wire!" I snapped at him. "I ain't wearing no damn wire on my body to go and see Papi. Are you crazy?"

"You wore one on me!"

"No the fuck I didn't! That's a damn lie."

"Look, Kira, I ain't trying to argue with you. 'Cause I know for a fact that the shit ain't gon' work if they don't get him on tape."

"Well, we're going to have a problem then because you and I both know how Papi and his people are. I would come up missing behind doing some shit like that. I mean, it's bad enough that I'm helping to set him up."

"But you ain't got a choice."

"What the hell you mean by that? I have a choice!"

"Listen to me, bitch!" Ricky screamed at me. "As of right now, your freedom to make choices just got revoked. Now I don't wanna hear nothing else about what you ain't gon' do, 'cause, you gon' do it. And if you don't, I swear on every one of my seeds that you and your cousin Nikki gon' come up missing. Y'all will get hunted down like dogs. And shit ain't gon' be nice. So you better think long and hard about whatcha saying because there ain't gon' be no turning back."

Now, before I could retaliate on this bastard, the time on his phone call expired. So I hung my phone up and lay my head back against the headrest of the office chair because I was pissed. And to have this piece of shit tell me that me and my cousin Nikki going to come up missing if I don't help him get Papi busted, bugged me the fuck out. He honestly just scared the hell out of me because I know for a fact, that there's people out here who owe him favors. So if and when any one of them are summoned, they will carry out his wishes without any questions asked.

What I got to do now is try to figure out a way to get out of this whole thing because either way it goes, I can get axed by Ricky's people or Papi's. I'm fucked all the way around the board. But, I do have one thing working for me and that is the fact that I have exactly one week to come up with a plan. So, I'm going to have to be very creative. And since I know I ain't gon' be able to do this alone, I'm forbidding myself from telling Nikki that her life is in danger. She would not know how to handle it. Somebody else is gonna have to come into play. And it's gon' have to be very, very soon.

GETTING MY SWAGGER ON

All last night Nikki begged me to ride with her, her friend Syncere, and some other guy out to Pentagon City for a little shopping trip. So this morning, I finally said I would go. And like a flash of lighting, she and her little entourage was parked outside of my apartment waiting patiently for me to come out.

Now Nikki had already given me the heads up on how good this other cat looked, and she had also told me that he looked like he had dough, too. So I was all for that. But what I liked most about her description of him is the part where she said he was tall, chocolate and handsome with a six-pack. And even though I ain't in the market for another man, ain't nothing wrong with going out with a cat when the tab is on him.

Before I walked out the house, I took one last look in the mirror that sat on the back of my bedroom door to make sure that the Christian Dior tank top and wrap-around skirt I was wearing looked spectacular around my curves. And once I realized that they were, I threw on my Christian Dior sunshades and made my exit.

When I got outside, I noticed all eyes were on me. And I loved it! It sent my confidence level about thirty feet in the air. I know I must've been working it.

Now once I stepped foot in Syncere's Range, Nikki immediately introduced me to him and his friend whom I sat next to in the back seat.

"Syncere and Mark, this is my favorite cousin Kira. Kira, this is my boo, Syncere, and his friend, Mark," she said.

We all spoke to each other in unison. And once Syncere got us on the highway, conversation time for Mark and I started up, even though Nikki and Syncere couldn't hear us. They were too busy up front talking over the blazing sounds of a Funkmaster Flex mix tape.

"You look real nice," Mark complimented.

"Thanks. And you don't look bad yourself," I replied as I began to admire his white-ass teeth. I mean, damn! Has he ever missed a dental appointment?

"And thank you," he said. "So, whatcha trying to cop at Pentagon City today?"

I smiled and said, "I don't know. But I could stand to get another Charles David handbag or a new pair of Bottega Veneta boots for the fall."

"You got cheese like that?"

"Nope. But I've got plastic," I told him.

"Well, maybe you won't have to use it."

"And what are my chances?"

"I can't say."

"And why not?"

"Because it all depends on what happens from now until we get there."

"So what, I've got to be on my best behavior?"

"No. I just want you to be yourself. Now, will that be hard?"

"Well, that won't be hard at all because I'm always being

myself. I can't see it any other way."

"So, where's your man?"

"I don't have one. But, I am on the verge of getting a divorce."

"Do you have any kids?" Mark wanted to know.

"No," I replied, refusing to let on that I was six weeks pregnant. "Do you?" I switched the question around to get the spotlight off me.

"No, I sho' don't."

"How old are you?"

"Thirty-one."

"Thirty-one! And you don't have any kids," I responded like I was surprised.

"Not that I know of."

"But you do have a woman, right?"

"Yeah, I got one."

"So, where is she now?"

"Probably at work."

"What does she do?"

"She goes to college."

"Which one?"

"Rutgers."

"Oh, so you live in New Jersey?"

"Sometimes."

"And where are you when you're not in Jersey?"

"I'm here with my peoples."

"Who, Syncere?"

"Yep."

"So, how long have you and your girl been together?"

"For about two years."

"Is y'all relationship serious?"

"It's what it is."

"And what does that mean?"

"It just means that we're together today. Who knows what tomorrow brings?"

"Oh, so you're on it like that?"

"I'm just living life, sweetheart. That's all," Mark told me in a sexy but roughneck kind of way, which turned me the fuck on. I mean, here I am, sitting next to this fly-ass nigga who appears to have a little bit of dough, and he just told me that he has a girl back home in New Jersey. Now, how gangsta is that? Because he could've lied. But he didn't. So I guess what they say is true: *Women are always attracted to cats who already got wives or girlfriends at home.* And I didn't get that from the *Hustler's Manual,* either.

So tell me, who wants to be with someone that nobody else wants? Which is why I'm just now realizing why I couldn't beat all of Ricky's hoes off with a stick. So if this cat right here got all the ingredients I like, then we can probably get into something. Shit! Who says he's got to be my man? I don't.

Our trip to Pentagon City didn't last long at all. All of a sudden, Syncere gets a fucking phone call while we were in Macy's, so we had to cut everything short. Nikki and I did manage to leave with two hot-ass handbags. Syncere copped her one by Salvatore Ferragamo and my new friend Mark copped me one by Charles David. He even let me throw in a belt because I agreed to go out with him tonight. I thought it was a fair exchange. And he did, too.

Now after we pulled up to my apartment, I got out of the truck and Mark got out right behind me so he could hand me my bags. The way he stood over me gave me the chills. And I mean in a good way, too. It reminded my of how Ricky used to stand next to me when he wanted to grab me up and fuck the hell outta me. So I was loving it. And the fact that he was beginning to make me feel like he was my protector, got me open. But nevertheless, I will still be on high alert with my heart. He won't get me off guard like Russ did. And that's a promise.

"What time you want to go out?" Mark asked me.

"Ummm," I began thinking to myself as I watched Nikki standing at the driver side door giving Syncere a goodbye kiss, "What about eight?" I finally said.

"Okay. I'll be back here at eight. So be ready," he commanded. Then he reached over and hugged me. I was about to fucking melt because this nigga's body felt good. And he smelled good on top of that. So there's no doubt in my mind that he's going to get this pussy.

Truly it is going to be a priority that I see what he's working with because, if the dick is good, then me and his other chick is going to have to share him. Shit! All the other scandalous hoes do it. And since I'm tired of being the nice one, it might be time for me to join their club.

"I'll be ready," I told him.

"A'ight," he said and then he hopped into the passenger seat of the truck and left.

Back in my apartment, Nikki took a seat on my couch, smiling from ear to ear. She couldn't stop talking about Syncere and the handbag he bought her.

"So, whatcha think?" she asked me.

"About what?" I played dumb.

"About Syncere."

"He's okay, I guess."

"His truck is hot, huh?"

"Yeah. It's nice," I agreed. But it wasn't all that, for real. I mean, anybody can add a navigational system and a couple of TVs to their whip. So, what's the big fucking deal?

"Can you see me and him together?" Nikki pressed on.

And even though I did not want to touch that subject, I got up the guts to answer her anyway, "Yes, but only if he doesn't start playing them stupid-ass games niggas be playing."

"Well, I think he's a pretty straight-up guy. So we'll probably be all right."

"I hope you're right. But just in case he does start flipping the script, have a backup plan. 'Cause nigga's like him, with money, always got some shit up their sleeves. So keep your eyes open."

"I will. But it probably won't be necessary. I mean, look at this," she instructed me, as she pointed to her new handbag. "I haven't ever had a guy buy me expensive shit like this, so there's got to be an interest somewhere."

"Look, I'm not saying that there isn't. All I'm saying is that you need to watch out for this guy because he got plenty of dough and trust me, them hoes out there in the street knows it. So come rain or shine, you're going to have some competition. And if you feel like he's worth fighting for, then you'd better get geared up 'cause them chickenheads out there don't care. They will get on their knees and suck your man's dick right in front of you, if they have to. So be prepared, is all I'm saying."

Nikki laughed at me as if I was telling her a joke. So I said to her, "You think it's a joke, huh?"

"No."

"Well, I hope not, 'cause this shit is for real. And clearly I would hate to fuck a bitch up behind you. But I will."

"Ahhhh..." she began to say as she got up from the couch to rush over to where I was standing. "I love you so much!"

"I love your crazy ass, too," I assured her as we both embraced one another.

"But you're going to stop falling in love so fast with these niggas out here, 'cause all of them ain't good for you."

"I know that."

"Well, you better act like it."

"I will. But let's get off of me for a second, 'cause I ain't the only one 'round with an expensive pocketbook."

"Whatcha talking 'bout?"

"You know what I'm talking about. I noticed how you were looking at Mark."

"And how was that?"

"Like you were falling in love or something."

"No, I wasn't," I said, and then I burst into laughter.

"Yes, you were. But it's okay, because Mark looks good as hell. As of matter of fact, he looks just like a taller version of Taye Diggs."

"I thought the same thing, too. And you know I love me some Taye Diggs."

"Yes. I know. So are you going to go out with him?"

"Yep. I sure am. And I'm going to make him take me to that new Italian restaurant off Laskin Road, too."

"Whatcha gon' wear?"

"Probably a cute little T-shirt and a pair of my Apple Bottom Capri jeans."

"Oh girl, you're really trying to start something because as soon as he sees you in those things, his dick is going to get hard as a rock."

"That's the idea," I commented and then I laughed.

"So can you see yourself messing around with him?" Nikki's questions continued.

"I don't know. But I've thought about it."

"Does he have a girlfriend?"

I sighed and said, "Yeah. But, she's back in Jersey, so she wouldn't be in the way at all."

"Does he have kids?"

"He said he doesn't."

"Must be nice, 'cause ol' Syncere got four of them running around."

"Well, damn!"

"And you can say that again. But I ain't going to sweat it, because all of 'em live back in New Jersey with their mamas, so I ain't got to deal with them," she replied, throwing her hands in the air as a sign of relief.

Anyway, we continued on chatting for about another hour or so. Then we settled down in my bedroom while I raided my closet for a hot pair of shoes to wear with my jeans. It took me some time, but with Nikki's help I finally pulled it together. So I'm going to look *ill* tonight.

GETTIN' IT POPPING

Mark called me from his cell phone and told me that he was about to pull up at my front door. So when he blew his horn, I grabbed the handbag he bought me earlier today and walked outside to meet him. And to my surprise, this nigga was sitting in the driver's side of a little-ass Ford Focus. I couldn't believe it! And I wanted so badly to make a U-turn and go right back in to my apartment, but I did make the deal to go out with him. Besides, it's not like I've got something else to do. So fuck it!

"Whose car is this?" I asked immediately after I got into the car.

"It's mine," Mark said with pride. "Why? What's wrong with it?"

"Don'tcha think it's a little too small for you?" I asked jokingly, even though I was serious as hell.

"Nah. It's just right," he replied and then sped off.

"So where we going?" Mark continued, giving me complete eye contact. And I mean, this cat was eyeballing me down, but I held my ground and stared back.

"Let's go to this new place off Laskin Road called Café Venice.

I heard their food is bananas!"

"Well, let's go then," he replied and then looked back at the road.

To make the mood of the drive more interesting, I got up the nerve to say, "Did you miss me?"

"Nah. But I been thinking 'bout cha, though."

"Ahhh, that's messed up!" I commented, nudging him in his arm.

"What's messed up about that? I just said that I been thinking about you."

"Well, because missing me and thinking about me are two totally different things. But since you said that you've been thinking about me, I would like for you to tell me what your thoughts were?"

"Well," Mark started saying, "I been thinking about how pretty you are."

"Oh, that's so sweet!"

"Wait! I ain't finished."

"Well, go 'head, then," I encouraged him.

"And I've been thinking about asking you to let me spend more time with you."

"You ain't got to ask me. 'Cause I'm sitting right here. And just so you know, if my company is ever needed by you, then I am there, okay?"

"A'ight," he replied, as he continued to drive us in the direction of the restaurant.

Now as soon as we got there, the hostess escorted us to our table, handed us menus and told us that our waiter will be with us in a minute. Mark took this time to look over his menu. I sat back in my chair to collect my thoughts, 'cause this nigga is looking good. I mean, his Caesar is tight with the light side burns all trimmed up nice, which makes his chocolate skin complexion look even better. Not to mention his skin is pimple free. He ain't even got a razor bump on his entire face. So trust me, this nigga is gorgeous and handsome as all get out. And that iced-out chain he got 'round his neck is only making matters worse for me.

I'm really starting to like this cat. Even though I know shit ain't going to jump off like I would want it to. And I'm just being realistic. I mean, come on now. Who am I kidding? This cat isn't going to want me after I tell him I'm pregnant with the next cat's baby. So there's no future with him. But I am going to enjoy his money and his company while it lasts 'cause I'm so tired of being lonely.

"So, what are you going to order?" I wanted to know.

"Probably this lasagna."

"Well, I'm going to order the Napoli shrimp Alfredo."

"Damn. That sounds good."

"I heard it was good, too." I replied and then our waitress walked up to take our order. We ran everything down to her and sent her on her way.

Meanwhile, Mark and I got into a more intense conversation.

"You said you didn't have a man, right?"

"Yes."

"Well, who be keeping you company at night?"

"My pillow. Why, you want the job or something?"

"Oh, I would love to get the job."

"Well, all you got to do is act right."

"Act right, huh?"

"Yep."

"How?"

"Just continue to keep it real with me. You know, how you did when I asked you if you had a girl and you told me yeah?"

He nodded.

"Okay, then, keep shit going strong like that. I don't care

90   *Kiki Swinson*

what it is. 'Cause I'ma do the same with you. That way we can avoid drama. God knows that I've had enough drama in my past with my soon-to-be ex-husband."

"Oh, stop fronting. You know you ain't gon' divorce that nigga."

"Yes, I am. I'm done with his trifling ass and his three baby mamas. Now, they can have each other. And I mean that."

"Does he be trying to call you?"

"Sometimes. But not as much as he used to. I guess he done caught the hint. 'Cause I told him, 'Don't call me! Call all them hoes you fucked around on me with.'"

"Damn! That's messed up!"

"Nah. What's messed up is the fact that he was fucking around behind my back with one of my hair stylists. Then later on, after he gets locked up, my house and a lot of my shit in it got seized and auctioned off by the government. Now I got to live in a little-ass condo. So you tell me who got the bad end of the stick?"

"Yeah. You got played. But you gon' be a'ight, beautiful. 'Cause I got faith in you," Mark told me, looking dead in my eyes once again. And that shit tore me up inside. Sparks started flying every damn where. And believe it or not, my pussy started tingling too. I guess me and him might have a connection going or something. The chemistry is about flow. I can feel it.

Now once our dinner date was officially over, which was around eleven o'clock, we rolled on back to my place. When we got there, I told him to make himself comfortable in the living room on the couch and watch some T.V. while I changed my clothes. And since I was on a mission to make him drool at the mouth, I slipped into my red coochie-cutter satin pajama shorts with the satin red top to match.

But when I went back into the living room to show off my

goodies, this nigga was knocked out, asleep. So I tried to wake him, but he wasn't budging. I guess all that Rémy he was sipping on at dinner really got his ass toasted. And now I'm just sitting here with nothing to do. I mean, he could have at least waited to go to sleep after he seen my sexy-ass PJs. Shit! I also wanted to give him a sneak preview. Ya know, sit on his lap, slob him down and let him grind on me a little bit, so I can see how big his dick gets when it's hard.

But I'm five minutes too late. Damn! What a fucking waste! Anyway, I got up and grabbed a blanket from out of my linen closet and laid it across him. And while I was doing this, his cell phone started chirping like crazy. But this nigga still wouldn't budge. So you know what I wanted to do? Yeah, I ain't going to front. I wanted to reach in his pocket and pull his cell phone right on out so I could see who was calling him this time of the night.

But I decided not to play myself because he could be testing me. Not only that, it's way too early in the game for that bullshit. So I left it alone. And then when I was about to walk away from him, I noticed that most of his money had fallen out of his pocket. Some of it was on the couch and the rest of it was on the floor. I picked all of it up. Every fifty and one-hundred-dollar bill was crisp, and looked like it had just came from out of a bank.

As I began to stack all the new bills together, I couldn't help but count them as I put them back in sequence. And when I was done, I ended up with was eighty-five hundred, which was crazy because this wasn't all the dough he had. I could see another stack of folded bills sticking right out of his pockets from where I was standing. And I'm thinking that from the thickness of the other stack, that it's got to be at least four g's.

But truthfully speaking, that's not what I need to worry myself with. What I need to do is worry about how in the hell I am going to get this dough back into his pockets, before he wakes up and finds this shit in my hands. Boy, there's no telling what he'll say or do. And I ain't trying to find out either because I want to spend some of this real soon. So you know I got to play my cards right.

Meanwhile, I am going to tuck this money up under his side and call it a night. That way he'll be able to see it as soon as he gets up. And that's just how it's going to be.

That next morning Mark got up before I did, and when he realized that he had fallen asleep on my couch and I was lying in my room in my own bed, I heard him and them big ass feet he got trotting back towards my bedroom.

So I pretended to still be asleep when he walked up to my bed and took a seat on the edge of it.

"Hey Kira," he whispered.

I went into actress mode and said, "Yeah," as I squinted my eyes like I was trying to adjust them to the light.

"I'm getting ready to bounce," he told me.

"What time is it?" I asked him, playing the role as I began to rub my eyes with the tip of my fingers.

"It's almost eight-thirty."

"Why you leaving so early?" I started pouting.

"Because I got some stuff to take care of."

"Well, when am I going to see you again?"

"I'll come back by here tonight, if you want me to."

"I would love for you to come back. But what time are you talking about?"

"I don't know. Maybe seven. Eight."

"That's a good time. I should be out my shop by then."

"Well, a'ight. But I'ma call you before I come, okay?"

"Okay," I said.

Now as soon as I gave him the green light, Mark patted me on my ass and then he stood up. So, my comment to him was, "Don't start nothin' you can't finish."

"Oh yeah," he replied smiling.

"Yeah," I said in a convincing manner.

"Well, we'll see about that later," he continued smiling and then he started stepping backwards in the direction of my bedroom door. I got up out of the bed and followed him. I felt like it would be very appropriate to walk him to the front door. But I also wanted to show him what he had missed out on last night.

So right before I was able to walk ahead of him, I pulled my satin shorts up a little bit more above my waistline so he could see my ass cheeks. And I made them jiggle too. Because after he leaves my house, I want him to think about my pretty, phat, round ass in between the times he's not thinking about business.

"You think I can get a kiss before you go?" I got up the nerve to ask before he got a chance to leave.

"Of course," Mark replied and planted a light kiss on my left cheek.

"What happened to the lip action?" I questioned him.

"Don't start nothin' you can't finish!" he threw right back at me and smiled and then he smacked me on the ass.

Smiling at his spontaneous tactic, I said, "Do that again and I'm gonna have to show you what you missed out on last night."

"Please don't tempt me," he urged me. "'Cause, if I didn't have to make this run, I would be on you right now. But, I will be back." His smile widened.

"Yeah, that's what your mouth say," I commented and watched him grab a hold of the doorknob.

Damn! That nigga got a nice-ass smile. Ol' fly muthafucka! Trying to act like he's a fucking gentleman and shit. Yeah, he's playing the role. And I'm loving it to death.

Upon his departure, I gave him a quick hug and sent him on his merry way 'cause the quicker he leaves, the sooner he'll be coming back.

PLAYING MY POSITION

"Wait right here while I open this door," C.O. Bivens instructed me when we approached this gold-painted steel door. So, I stood to the side and let her work her magic with them keys and with the click of the lock, we were on the other side in two seconds flat.

Now this room was beginning to make a nigga feel claustrophobic, but then again, it can't be no worse than that cramped-ass spot me and my cellmate gotta sleep in. And besides, how can I complain when I got this bad-ass chick standing in here next to me.

Yeah. It's just me and her, all by ourselves, at two-thirty in the morning, and I ain't even gotta wear the handcuffs. How sweet is that?

"Here, take your food," she continued, handing me a white Styrofoam box she pulled from behind a stack of boxes on the shelf behind us.

"What's in it?"

"The steak you wanted."

"Where did you get it from?" I asked her while I opened the container. I couldn't wait to see what I was about to eat because the shit the jail keeps feeding me goes right through me. And not only that, the shit is straight garbage.

"I stopped by the IHOP on the way here. So it still should be hot," she explained as she sat down on a case of ammonia.

I sat down right beside her but I gave her some space. I didn't want her to think that I was going to attack her or something. I'm too fly for that shit!

"Hurry up and eat, because Ms. Thomas will probably come looking for me in the next thirty minutes or so," Bivens continued.

"But she might not," I said after shoving a huge chunk of steak into my mouth.

"You might be right. But I don't want to take any chances."

"A'ight. That's cool," I told her. "But did my man Black give you everything you needed?"

"Yeah. But you know what? He gave me more money than I asked for."

"What he give you?"

"Four hundred."

"Oh, that's 'bout right."

"So you told him to give me that much?"

"Yeah. 'Cause I figured you could use it to get your hair and nails done or something."

"Thanks. That was really nice of you to do that for me."

"Look, Bivens...," I began, but she cut me off in mid-sentence and said, "My name is Lena."

"Okay, Lena. I told you that you could get anything you want from me. But I ain't gon' know what it is, until you ask me."

"I know. But a girl in my position can't just jump out of every moving car. You see, I have a job to do here. And it's against the rules to show favoritism to any of the inmates. So all of the correctional officers are instructed to treat y'all like has-beens. And sometimes it's easy. But with you, it was difficult."

"Why is that?" I asked feeling all happy and shit, like I'm a Don.

"Because you're different than they are."

"And how is that?" I kept egging her on. Shit, I need some ego boosting.

"Look, Ricky, if you must know, I heard about you on the streets way before you came up in here, thanks to my best friend, Lacy. She keeps up with all the ballers who live around town. And I know you probably don't remember this but right after the New Years, you and some other guy came by the Broadway on a Friday night to a birthday party for my best friend's sister, Ramona. You were wearing this gorgeous fur coat. And your friend was wearing a pretty red and blue leather jacket."

"Yeah, I remember that party," I told her right before I sipped on the cold soda she had bought me to go with my meal. "But I don't remember you being there," I continued, after I let out a burp.

"Now, how could you? When there were over a hundred other women there trying to get your attention." She ended with a big smirk on her face.

"Nah, I don't remember it being like that."

"Oh yes, you do. And you were loving it, too, because you were smiling your butt off."

"No, I wasn't," I said and then I smiled 'cause she wasn't lying. I was loving the hell out of all that attention them hoes were showing me. I mean, what man wouldn't?

"Tell me something," Lena came back at me.

"What's up?"

"How many of those women did you and your friend take to the hotel with you that night?"

"None of them. I ain't want them. Shit! You want to know the truth? I wish I would've ran across you that night."

"And what would have happened if you did?"

Aaahhh man! Now I got to go into pimp mode, 'cause this chick is throwing questions at me full force. And from the tone of her voice, she sounds like she's in the mood to hear me say some real good shit to her. So I finally came out and told her what she wanted to hear.

"I would've took you out to dinner. And then we probably would've went to see a movie."

"So you wouldn't have tried to play me?"

"Play you how?" I asked, even though I already knew where she was going with this question.

"I'm talking about how most men skip out on women after they get what they want from them."

"Well, that ain't my style. And it damn sho' wouldn't be with you 'cause Lena, you got it going on. So I want to make sho' you keep it that way."

"And how will you make the effort to do that?"

"You let me worry about that part. You just continue doing what I need you to do," I told her.

"I will," she replied in her cute little voice.

Now since I knew the clock was still ticking, I hurried up and finished eating my food, and then right after I finished up my soda, I handed everything back to her.

"Was it good?" she asked me.

"Ya damn right! But next time, tell them don't cook it so hard."

"Okay," she replied and then started stuffing everything in this black trash bag.

"You ready?" she continued, which was the wrong question

because I wasn't ready to go back to that dirty-ass cell block. And plus, I wanted some pussy. Or at least see it for that matter. So I said, "Damn, you trying to get rid of me already?"

"No. But remember, we're not trying to blow this."

"A'ight. A'ight. But can I at least get a kiss or something?" I suggested because a nigga like me was grasping for straws.

"All right, but just one kiss."

I stood up 'cause I got happy as hell. And when I leaned over to lay a wet one on her lips, she met me halfway and that's when our lips locked. And boy, was I feeling it. My dick started feeling it, too.

I slid my tongue in her mouth and threw my arms around her waist. Now, I thought she was gon' push me away, but she didn't. So I pulled her closer to me 'cause I wanted her to feel my big missile against her pussy. And as soon as I did it, fireworks shot off every muthafucking where.

My dick pressed against her pussy was about to send me up the fucking wall. And I could tell that she was about to go with me because this chick started grinding on me. So I started grinding back. And then our kisses started going in slow motion with me tugging on her bottom lip. But I couldn't stop there, 'cause my dick was 'bout to explode.

That's when I said, "Fuck it!" and grabbed both of her ass cheeks in the palm of my hands and pulled her even closer to me, so I could grind on her harder.

Then, out of nowhere, this chick started acting like a beast and started tugging on my jumpsuit.

"Take it off," she instructed me in a low whisper, as she started kissing me on my neck.

So without giving it a second thought, I let her ass go and came right on out of my suit. I was standing there wearing nothin' but a pair of white boxers, with my dick trying to bust through the open slit in the front. After Lena noticed how tight my six-pack was, she grabbed for my dick and started massaging it. And boy, I was about to jump the fuck outta my skin. I reached over and started feeling on her titties. Damn! These muthafuckas is soft as hell. And I can feel how hard her nipples are, too. But I wanna see them.

I started unbuttoning her shirt. And that's when she jumped back.

"Wait! No!" she stuttered.

Since I wasn't trying to hear that, I said, "What's wrong?"

"Let me just suck your dick," she told me. And even though I was gamed for that, that wasn't gon' be enough. So I came back and said, "Nah, Lena. Let me fuck you."

"I can't."

"Why?" I asked desperately. If she didn't hurry up, my dick was gon' go limp on me, and I wasn't trying to let that happen. I've got too much pressure built up right now.

"Because we don't have a condom."

"Look baby, I promise I'll pull out."

"That isn't what I'm worried about."

"Look, sweetheart," I began to plead, "Ain't nothin' wrong with me. And I ain't got that AIDS shit either. So you ain't got to worry about it. I promise."

Now before she gave me an answer, I kicked a little bit more game and said, "And so that you know, if I didn't give a fuck about cha, I would've just let you suck my dick and carried your ass. But see, I'm carrying it different with you. Shorty, I like you a whole lot. And that's why I'ma make sure that you get taken care of. That's my word!"

Lena thought about what I said because after she let out a long sigh, she said, "All right. But please pull out before you cum."

"I will, baby. You got my word," I replied, happy as a muthafucka, massaging my dick 'cause he was on the verge of becoming Mr. Softy. But, with a couple of strokes, I had him back up and running.

"Turn around," I instructed her, after she pulled her pants down below her knees. And when she did that, I finally got to see how pretty and round her ass is. The shit is perfect! It's so damn beautiful that my dick started jumping, which made me get even more excited. So I bent her over, moved her thong strap to the side and went straight in for the kill. I dove in headfirst. And it was like, the second I stuck my dick in her wet, juicy pussy, feelings I thought I ain't ever had started coming out of the woodworks. The shit was so strong, it went straight to my heart. It was fucking bananas! And it seemed like with each stroke, the feelings in my dick started taking over my whole body.

And then on top of that, she started throwing the pussy back on me. So being the big dawg I am, I had to take control and hold shit down. And that's when I laid the pipe down and started pumping it in her real good. So believe me, she was feeling it in her stomach because she started moaning her ass off, saying, "Ooooh...Ricky! Fuck this pussy, baby. Yeah, do it just like that!"

Now I'm about to give you some real shit, 'cause after hearing this chick moaning and telling me to keep beating her pussy up, I was getting hyper. So after a dozen more strokes, I exploded. And I did keep my word and pulled out on her. But I made her wear every last bit of this protein in the crack of her ass. I also beat my dick on her cheeks, so I could see her ass jump some more. Plus, I wanted to make sho' I got a chance to release every drop of it. And guess what? I did. But I was weak as hell after I let my shit off. And it's all gravy, 'cause I just got me some pussy. So I'm straight now.

"C'mon, let's get out of here," she said as she started zipping up her pants.

"You a'ight?" I asked her even though I didn't really give a fuck.

"Yes, I'm okay," she told me and then she kissed me on the mouth. "I just want to hurry up and get you back to the block before someone comes looking for me."

"Well, a'ight. I'm ready," I replied and then I tapped her on her ass. "I'ma have my man Black holla at you tomorrow, okay?"

"Okay."

"Oh yeah," I came back at her. "I heard that trustee nigga tried to holla at you yesterday."

"Who, Kelsey?"

"Yeah, him."

"Oh, he's harmless. And I never pay him any mind."

"That's cool. But you need to straighten that shit out before I have something done to his punk ass."

"All right," Lena replied and then she unlocked the supply room door. Back to the block I went.

ANYTHING -4- PROFIT

Since we have passed the dinner and a movie stage, Mark invited me to hang out with him at a dog fight tonight, which is a major gambling spot for him. When I accepted his invitation, he told me to be ready to leave the crib by ten p.m. And once Nikki got word that Syncere was going to be there as well, she happily volunteered herself to accompany us along for the ride.

"So, where is this dog fight suppose to be at?" Nikki asked from the back seat.

Now, being as though I wasn't driving and was unaware of our destination, I let Mark answer her question. "In P-town, Portsmouth, VA, at this spot ran by this old dude."

"So what happens at a dog fight?" Nikki continued.

"It's just a spot where a whole bunch of niggas gather around and watch two pits go at each other's asses.

"That's it?" Nikki replied in a disappointing manner.

"Yeah, if you ain't got money in the pot."

"Oh, so y'all be gambling off that shit?" Her questions continued.

"Nah. It's called eating!" Mark began to explain. "That's how a lot of niggas be getting it these days."

"Does Syncere bet too?" she wanted to know.

"Big time. That nigga goes hard at these fights."

"Well, I sure hope he wins tonight. Because I could sure use a new paint job on my car."

"I know that's right!" I agreed in a humorous fashion.

The ride to this back wood section of P-town was centered around a lot of farm land. It had to be every bit of thirty acres of wooded area. We traveled down a long, dirt road, without a street light in sight, that led us to this rundown-looking warehouse with an assortment of late-model whips and SUVs. Once Mark found a parking space, Nikki and I were on our way to see what was behind door number one.

Immediately after we were let in through the double steel doors, a thick cloud of smoke grabbed me right by the throat and choked the hell out of me. It seemed like every cat in there was puffing on something or another, which became an instant turn-off for me, but I kept my mouth shut. The last thing I wanted to do was start complaining. Tonight is Mark's night, so I am going to let him do him.

Moments later, Mark escorted us to a set of bleachers surrounded by a small fenced-in ring, which I am assuming was where the dogs would fight.

"Y'all sit right here while I go put my bet in," he told us and then he disappeared into a crowded corner in the opposite side of the warehouse.

"I wonder how much money he's getting ready to put up?" I said aloud, awaiting a response from Nikki.

"Shit! I don't know. But from the looks of the cats walking around here, it ain't going to be chump change."

Instead of commenting, I giggled because I was suddenly beginning to agree with her assumption. The niggas that were parading around here look like they got it going the fuck on, sporting their beautiful jewels, fresh whites (D.C.'s or Uptowns or Air Force Ones), as the others utilized their T-Mobile Side-kicks to send out a few text messages.

"Oooh, look at him," I insisted, making reference to this tall cat with caramel skin and chiseled features, rocking a multi-colored, pin striped RocaWear button-down shirt and a crisp pair of blue jeans with the Roc label branded on his right back pocket. Nikki and I both could see how magnificent and de-fined his physique was, with the white tank top tightly fitted and nestled against his six pack. He wore nothing else of value, except a blinged-out watch. We could not catch the inscription of the designer's name, because we were too far away. But we could tell that the design and the number of diamonds were put together beautifully. So to sum it all up, *yes,* Nikki and I would both fuck home boy. He's definitely our type, among a few others swarming around here like they were looking for a date.

"I wonder where Syncere is? Because I don't see him any-where," Nikki said.

"He's probably over there in that crowd of niggas, placing his bet like everybody else," I told her.

And once again my intuition was correct because about four or five minutes later, Mark reappeared before us with Syncere right by his side.

"Look who I found?" Mark commented as he took a seat next to me.

"What's good!" Syncere greeted.

I smiled and nodded my head while Nikki said, "Hey, baby!"

Syncere responded to Nikki with a kiss on the lips and then he took a seat next to her. Other attendees followed suit and took their seats as the bell sounded for the fight to began.

Moments later, the fight between a red-nosed female pit

bull and a male brindled pit bull began, after they were placed inside the ring and released by their owners.

"Oh, shit!" I yelled after I witnessed the red-nosed pit bull locked into the other pit bull's neck with at least two hundred pounds of pressure.

"Yeah! Get 'em!" Mark yelled with excitement.

While I heard Syncere, as well as a few others, cheer for the other dog, Nikki sat back in a bewildered kind of way and remained quiet. And in just a matter of minutes, it became apparent that this dog fight episode wasn't for her. It's probably due to the fact that she was a dog lover. But on the other hand, I was personally fascinated by it.

Seeing two pits trying to rip each other apart is like an adrenaline rush. It's like being with your man, watching him pull out his pistol after somebody tries to disrespect him. It's kind of exciting, to say the least.

The fight lasted for about five minutes with the red–nosed one coming out as the winner. She was a beast. Oh boy, did that make Mark's day.

"Oh yeah, baby! We celebrating tonight!" Mark commented as he stood up.

"Sounds good to me," I replied and then I stood up as well.

"I don't believe this shit!" Syncere blurted out and then he sighed heavily.

"Don't cry now. I told you to put your dough on the *bitch*!" Mark began to remind him.

"Man, I ain't trying to hear that bullshit! Especially not after all that money I just lost."

"Stop fucking with that nigga, Monty, and you won't be 'round here losing cheese like that."

"Yeah. What the fuck ever!" Syncere replied and then he abruptly walked off, leaving Nikki standing there with us.

"How much did he lose?" Nikki asked Mark.

"Twenty grand."

"You're lying, right?" she asked in disbelief.

"Nah, I don't lie about money," he commented and then he turned to me and said, "Let me run over here so I can cash in."

"A'ight. Go 'head," I insisted.

Immediately after he walked away, I turned to Nikki and said, "I wonder how much he won?"

"Well whatever it is, it's a fucking lot!"

"You think I should ask him?" I asked her.

"Shit! Why not? I mean, I would have asked Syncere if he was sitting in the winners seat. And speaking of which, I wonder if he already left?"

"I don't think he'll leave you here."

"Girl, please, that muthafucka has been acting really crazy these last few days. Yesterday I wanted so badly to ask him if he was on his period after he screamed at me for forgetting to clean my hair out of the bathroom sink."

"Oh, well, I don't fault the man for screaming at you behind that. You know I don't play that, either."

"No shit!" Nikki commented sarcastically and then she smiled.

"Come on. Let's walk over here," I said changing the subject.

"All right. But let me call Syncere on his cell and find out where he's at," Nikki replied as she retrieved her cellular phone from the clip on her hip.

I took a few steps back away from her in hopes of giving her a little privacy. But guess what? I could still hear her conversation.

"Where you at?" I heard her say. And then a couple of seconds later she said, "A'ight. Well, I'm on my way," she continued and then ended the call.

"He's still here, huh?" I wasted no time in asking.

"Yeah. He's outside waiting for me to come out."

"Well, was he going to call you and tell you that?"

"I guess not."

"Oh yeah, then he is tripping."

"I told you."

"Well, go ahead. And I'll catch up with you later."

"All right. Call me in the morning."

"Okay. I love you."

"I love you, too," Nikki assured me and walked off.

It only took about fifteen more minutes for the bookie to pay Mark his dough. When all the formalities were laid down, my baby grabbed me into his arms and we were out of there.

On the way back to my place, I went into *Girl 6* mode and started talking really freaky to Mark, who by this time couldn't keep his eyes on the road because of how hard I was tugging at the zipper on his jeans.

"Whatcha doing?" he asked me as I began to massage his dick.

"I'm getting ready to give you some head," I boldly replied.

"You sho' you ready for that?"

"I was born ready," I told him, gradually peeling away the layers of his jeans and boxer shorts, which landed me the surprise I was waiting for.

Pulsating from top to bottom, I was holding all eight inches of his big black dick. And like a kid in a candy store, I picked it up and greedily put it into my mouth.

"Ahhhh shit!" Mark said, the moment he felt the pleasurable effects of my mouth taking his hard dick in like shelter. I had engulfed every inch I could muster without choking on it.

"Oh yeaaaaah," he continued as I stroked the shaft of his penis in a rhythmic motion with my right hand, but giving myself enough room to grace the head with my tongue. And then, like the kid in me, I slammed dunk that hard meaty pipe right back into my mouth.

"Mmmmmm...," I said between licks, "This dick tastes so good!"

"Well, eat it up, baby! Eat it up!" Mark moaned.

And like the submissive woman I am, I did just that. Holding his entire dick in both hands, I began to tease the tip of the head with my tongue like I was licking a lollipop. Then I put it in my mouth halfway, but released it with a light grip, trying not to apply too much pressure because I wanted him to savor the moment.

"Damn girl, you sucking this dick real good!" he exclaimed, and in turn gave me my props for setting shit off in the right way. The connection was there, so to heighten the pleasure of our engagement, I pulled my mouth back up to the tip and tightened my mouth around the head, then I released it to stroke the shaft while I consumed his nut sack into my mouth.

"Mmmmmmm," I said once again, still stroking the hell outta his thick pipe. And sho'nuff, after working my mouth for about ten minutes, like it was my pussy, Mark grabbed a hold of my head for dear life. I got truly excited by this, which was a clear indicator that my mouth was working magic. Plus, the juices from my pussy were running their course of saturating my panties, so you know I was ready to fuck the shit out of this nigga the minute we stepped foot through the front door of my apartment.

"Ahhhh...baby, I'm about to cum!" he warned me as he closed his eyes to concentrate his way to a climax.

"Go 'head baby, cum in my mouth," I demanded, taking in every bit of manhood he had to offer me.

"Aaaaaaaaaaah...," he finally yelled, as the grip on my head got tighter.

And before I knew it his dick exploded like a cannon, shooting a warm milky solution into my mouth and I welcomed every drop of it. I couldn't afford to waste any of it. I wanted him to see that I wanted him in the worst way and it worked like a charm, because after he let out a long sigh, Mark said, "Goddamn, girl, where the hell you been at all my life?"

I wiped my mouth with a Popeye's Chicken napkin I found next to the cup holder and said, "I don't know, but I'm here now."

I sat back up in the seat, waiting to go for round two at my place.

HOES GALORE

My morning was off to a real good start. Because after I whipped my pussy and that good ol' head I got on Mark, he got up and fixed me breakfast. Now Ricky ain't never did no shit like this for me. So you know I was cheesing my ass off when Mark served me a plate of maple turkey sausages, cheese eggs and toast. Shit, after that meal, I fucked around and gave him some more head 'cause he damn sho' deserved it.

But it seemed like the very second we parted ways, everything started falling down around me. The moment I pulled up on the premises of my salon, I noticed Rhonda outside in the parking lot swinging on her baby daddy, Tony.

I immediately parked my car and hopped out to see what the hell they were fighting for while all of our clients and the other stylists were looking out the window at their stupid asses.

"What's up y'all? What are y'all doing?" I rushed over to Tony's car and asked.

"This dirty muthafucka was out fucking that nasty bitch, Letisha, I was telling you about," Rhonda explained between each shortened breath, as she held onto huge chunks of Tony's white tee with both of her hands.

"Oh, so you be telling Kira our business, huh?" Tony shouted out at her.

"Look," I interjected, "Y'all need to stop that. People are out here watching y'all make damn fools of yourself."

"Fuck them! I don't care because I'ma kill this nigga today. And I mean it."

When Rhonda said that, I knew right then and there that she meant that shit. I could also see the pain in her eyes. So I walked up to the both of them and grabbed a hold of her arm and said, "Rhonda, girl, I know you're mad. But don't be letting everybody all in your business. Look at all them hoes in the shop watching y'all. You know they laughing and shit."

"That's what I been trying to tell her, but she ain't listening," Tony yelled , as if he was real frustrated.

"Shut up! You cheating ass bastard! I'm just so sick of your fucking games," Rhonda shouted back.

"Come on, girl," I said, trying to pull her in my direction. But she wouldn't budge. So I said, "Rhonda, there's a better way to handle this. So let him go."

"Yeah, let me go, wit'cha stupid ass!"

"Fuck you!" Rhonda flipped out and sucker punched him dead in the middle of his temple. Tony punched her ass right back. And when he hit her, she lost her balance and fell back on the ground.

"I told you to keep your hands off me," he yelled once he was able to get a few feet away from her. "Now, look at 'cha!" He scrambled to get into his car.

Right after I reached down to help her get back on her feet, she placed her hand over her forehead and said, "I'm leaving your nothing ass! You lil' dick muthafucka'! 'Round here acting like you holding. Nigga, you ain't holding nothin' but a pocketful of nuts. You punk bitch!"

"Yeah. What the fuck ever!" Tony yelled again from the driver side window of his car. "Because I'm gon' leave your dumb ass first. I'm tired of your bullshit! Running around chick's houses, busting windows and shit, with my muthafucking kids in the backseat of the car, watching your stupid ass! Yo, you lucky I told her not to go outside and beat cha ass!"

"You should've, you crab-ass pussy! Calling yourself a drug dealer, with your broke ass. You ain't no hustler, for real! Because ain't nobody giving your ass no packs. Yeah. They know your clown ass gon' fuck they shit up. That's why Bink stopped calling you back. Yeah, I know what time it is."

"You don't know shit! You dumb bitch!" Tony continued to retaliate until he put his car in gear and sped off out of the parking lot.

Rhonda just stood there, in a daze, with teardrops falling from her eyes. And since I couldn't stand to see her like this, I grabbed her by the hand and walked her on over to my car. I figure this would be a better place to talk.

Now after we got in and took a seat, I opened up and said, "So, you caught his ass at that girl's house, huh?"

"Yeah," she replied as she began to wipe the tears away from her face.

"What time did you catch him over there?"

"It was still dark. So it was about four-thirty this morning."

"What exactly did you do when you went there?"

"Well, when I seen his car parked outside her apartment, I got out my car and knocked on her door since he wouldn't answer his cell phone. But she refused to come to her own door. So I started kicking it."

"You did?" I asked, surprised.

"Yep. I sho' did. And then I started cussing real loud so all her neighbors could hear me. That's when some old lady from next door stuck her head out of her window and said she was gon' call the police if I didn't leave. So, right after I told her to mind her fucking business, I threw a brick right through Letisha's front room window and left."

I couldn't help but bust into laughter after Rhonda just gave me the rundown about what she had done. So instead of coming down hard on her about how wrong she was for doing what she did, I said, "Are you going to be all right?"

"Kira," she sighed, "I am so tired of dealing with his shit. I mean, all the stuff I done been through with him done broke me down. And right now, I don't know if I'm coming or going."

"So have you figured out what you're going to do about your relationship?"

"Girl, I'm done. I can't take it no more. So he's got to go."

"So you're putting him out?"

"Hell, yeah! That nigga is getting outta my house tonight."

"Are you sure that's what you want to do? I mean, I know how it is when you want your man gone. But, then after everything cools down, you start feeling different."

"Yeah, I know. But I'm serious this time. Because if I let this mess he did go, he ain't gon' do nothin' but do it again. Now ain't that how they all do it?"

"You're definitely right about that one," I agreed.

"Well, now, you see where I'm coming from." Rhonda looked back down her watch.

"Do you feel like going back to work?"

"Nah. Not really. But I've got three clients under the dryer and one in the chair. So I've got to."

"No, you don't. I can do them if you want me to."

"Nah. It's okay. I got it," she insisted.

"Well, just sit here in my car for a few minutes until I

straighten things out in the shop."

"A'ight," she agreed.

Now before I entered the salon, I took a deep breath because I knew the moment I walked through this door, there was going to be a whole lot of questions. I immediately prepared myself.

"Hello, ladies," I spoke the second I stepped through the door.

"Hey," everyone replied in unison.

"Anybody called me?" I asked aloud for the entire salon to hear.

"Yeah," April replied. "Some man named Burgess called. He said he was your husband's lawyer and that he needed you to call him back, because it's really important that he speak with you. So I wrote his number down and stuck it on your desk in the back office."

"Okay. Thanks," I said as I began to feel my heart pick up speed. I know what he wants. That's why his ass is going to wait until I'm good and ready to call him back.

"Did anybody else call me?"

"No," April replied once again, as she walked up to my station. "But where's Rhonda? Is she alright?"

"She's sitting in my car. And yes, she's alright. But please leave her be when she comes back in the shop. She's got too much shit on her mind right now to be answering a whole lot of questions."

"Okay, I understand. So I won't say nothin' to her."

"Good. But let me ask you something."

"What?"

"Tell me who was running their mouth when all that drama was going on outside?"

"I didn't hear nobody say nothin'. But I did hear a couple of your clients laughing when she fell on the ground after he hit her."

"Yeah. A'ight," I said because I really didn't believe her. But since I didn't have a choice in the matter, I'm going to deal with it and leave it alone because the hoes up in here can get fake at the drop of a dime. So I know I'm going to always have to deal with the bitter and the sweet.

Right when I was about to set the security alarm for the shop, it dawned on me that I hadn't call Mr. Burgess back. I took a couple steps backwards and grabbed the cordless phone from off my station and dialed his number.

"Hello," he said immediately after the lines of communication opened up.

"Hello, Mr. Burgess. This is Kira."

"Hi. How are you?"

"I'm fine. Now what can I do for you?" I got straight to the point.

"Well, I just wanted to let you know that I spoke with the federal investigators earlier today, and they are requesting to have a meeting with you, since you're going to assist them with their investigation on Papi and his men."

"So when did they say they wanted to see me?"

"They didn't say, exactly. But they are pressing for one day next week, if that's okay with you."

"Next week is fine. Get back with me when they give you the heads up on what it's going to be."

"Well, they were saying that it would be better if you decided upon one."

"But I can't do that right now because I've got a couple of appointments scheduled for next week. And I would run them down to you, but I left my organizer back at my apartment."

"Well, will you be able to call me back with that information by tomorrow?"

"I'll try," I said in a nonchalant manner.

"Okay, then. Well, I guess that's settled," he commented sarcastically.

"Yeah. A'ight. Whatever!" I replied.

Right when he was about to hang up, he said, "Kira, I've got one last thing to ask you...if you don't mind."

"And what is that?"

"Do you really want to help your husband?"

"No. Not really."

"But you will, right?"

"Yeah," I replied and then I let out a long sigh.

"Okay. Well, do you have another contact number? Because it's really hard trying to get through to you at your hair salon."

"Well, I'm sorry that I'm hard to get in touch with, but I don't have another phone number. So you gon' have to keep trying to reach me here," I told him in a candid way.

Once he realized that I would only help him and Ricky on my terms, he saw that there was no use in continuing with this conversation, so he said his goodbyes and hung up.

Now I betcha after he hung up, he was calling me all kinds of names, but who gives a damn? Because I sure don't!

HATERS WILL HATE

My cellmate Bossman just pulled my jacket about the talk that's going around in some of the cell blocks concerning me and Lena. I sat back on my bunk and listened to what he had to say.

"Yo, dawg! Mu'fuckas 'round this joint gotcha on the radar and they trying to stop your show with C.O. Bivens. So you better start watching your back," he told me.

"Goddamn! How niggas found out 'bout that? Shit! It ain't even been a week yet since I started fucking with her."

"C'mon Ricky, look where we at? You know somebody is always peeping shit out."

"So who told you this?" I wanted to know.

"That nigga Dune from the trustee block."

"Damn! I wonder how he found out?"

"I don't know. But he also told me that most of the niggas 'round here know she be bringing you plenty of shit in here from off the streets. And right now, they straight hating on you, dawg."

"Fuck 'em, na mean?"

"Yeah, but don't sleep on them."

"So, whatcha think I should do?"

"I don't know, dawg. But you gon' have to be real crafty with this one."

"Do you think that nigga Dune will tell you which niggas got me on the radar?"

"C'mon Ricky, you know damn well you can get anything you want for the right price."

"Well, step to that nigga and see what his price is for that information and let me know. 'Cause I want whoever's talking mouths to get wired."

"Oh yeah, for the right price, I can make that happen, too."

"Good. Because I'm about to put some shit in motion that'll keep me and you paid in here. So I can't let none of them crab-ass niggas interfere with that! And not only that, home-girls pussy is crazy good, so I ain't ready to let nobody interfere with that, either."

Bossman laughed at my comment and said, "Damn, dawg. Is the pussy good like that?"

"Yeah, man. That shit is popping! And it's always wet, too."

"I betcha be tearing it up. Dontcha?"

"You damn right! Every chance I get. But what's so crazy is, when we first got together, she wanted to suck my dick instead of giving me some pussy. But I was like, nah. I wanna fuck. So then she was like, '*but we ain't got a condom.*' So you know I had to kick game to her, 'cause I was not about to let her walk out of that room without giving me the goods. So I told her, '*I'll pull out.*' And she went for it.

"That's what's up!" Bossman agreed with me and then he said, "But, tell me what wheels you trying to put in motion? 'Cause if you talking 'bout that venture we were speaking about a few weeks ago, then I'm all geared up and ready."

"Yeah," I started saying, "I talked to my peoples on the outside and they gon' send us some good shit up in here. And I'm talking 'bout shit that's gon' have these mu'fucka's 'round here looking like *zombies*."

"Oh, yeah. We gon' need something like that."

"That's what I was telling my peoples. And because that shit is so lethal, we going to be able to spread it around and blow up."

"So when are you trying to do this?" he asked me.

"Very soon, baby boy! Very soon!" I assured him. 'Cause I wasn't gon' tell him exactly when my pack was going to make landfall. It ain't good to let the next man know your every move. I mean, even Bossman know that. But I guess since I only been kicking it with him since my bid started, he thinks that I'm on it like that with him.

And don't get me wrong, 'cause he's a cool dude, but I've got to protect my investment. And that's some real shit!

I got another letter from Sunshine today talking about she ain't heard from the appeals court, which is a good sign that they'll grant her the appeal. But I wasn't trying to hear that shit. I don't want to hear about nobody getting out of jail but me. So fuck all that other shit!

And then her letter started talking 'bout how much she misses and loves me. But that ain't nothin' but game. I know she's telling me this 'cause she wants my peoples to keep sending her dough, so her commissary can stay tight.

Yeah. She thinks I'm stupid. But it ain't that type of party with us no more. I mean, it ain't like she can do something for me. I can't get no pussy or head from her. So what good is she to me now? Not a damn thing! So I'm going to dead this pen pal thing with her real soon. She's done.

Later that night I woke up to the sounds of some bitch-ass nigga moaning 'cause some punk was sucking him off. Now this type of shit makes me sick to my damn stomach when I hear these niggas acting like a man and a woman. But as soon as the lights come on, the same ones be 'round here patrolling like they soldiers or something. That's why I wish one of them would ever run up on me with that bitch shit! 'Cause when they do, I'ma straight put 'em out of their misery! Ol' con-fused-ass muthafuckas!

NOTHIN'S -4-EVER

Rhonda called me early this morning and woke me out of my sleep to tell me she wasn't going to be coming into shop today.

"But why?" I asked because it's not like her to miss any days, especially when I know she has a long list of clients' hair that needs to be done today.

"Because I am too emotionally drained right now to be around anybody, that's all."

"What's wrong?"

She sighed and said, "I just got some unfinished business to talk to Tony about."

"Where is he?"

"He just called me about twenty minutes ago and said that he was on his way here. And he thinks I'm stupid, too, but I bet you any amount of money that he's coming from Letisha's house. 'Cause when I asked him where he was at, he tells me that he was just leaving his mama's house. So after we hung up, I called Ms. Mable and she told me that she ain't seen or talked to Tony in two days. Now you tell me what you think?"

"Well, it's obvious. The nigga lied. And now he's going to come home with more lies. So don't fall for that shit, girl."

"I'm not. But I am gon' sit back and hear what he's got to say. I mean, you should've heard him begging me to let him come back home. Talking about how sorry he is for hurting me. And that he ain't gon' do it no more because he sees how it's affecting out kids."

"And what did you say?"

"I told him that we need to sit down and put everything on the table and work it out from there."

"C'mon now, Rhonda. Girl, you know that shit he's talking about ain't nothing but game. I mean, look how many times this nigga done screwed around on you already. He's not going to change and you know it."

"But we don't know that, for real."

"Yes, we do. So please stop lying to yourself."

"But...," Rhonda began saying.

I interjected and said, "But nothing, Rhonda! This man of yours disrespects you and hits you in public. Now are you gonna sweep that under the rug? 'Cause if you do, trust me, it's going to happen over and over again, just like all that other fucked-up shit he does to you."

"So, you wouldn't let him come back?"

"That's not for me to say. But I will say this—stop short-changing yourself, because you deserve a whole lot better. And I know you can be so much happier if you just let all that baggage go."

"You're right."

"Okay. So if I'm right, then whatcha gon' do when that nigga come walking through the front door?"

"I don't know."

"Oh, you know! It's just that you're afraid of going on with

your life without him being in the picture. You're so used to
having him around, so you're not sure if you can function without him. But you can, if you just stop letting him consume you
with all his drama."

"Kira, it's not that easy."

"Rhonda, I know it's not. But it'll get easier every time you
take a step forward. You see, I did it."

"Yeah. And that was because Ricky got locked up."

"Okay. And you're right. But, do you see me running down
to the jail to visit him?"

"No."

"Exactly. And that's because I could care less about his no-
good ass! You remember all the shit he used to put me through?"

"Yeah."

"But guess what?"

"What?"

"He will never be able to drag me through that bullshit
again."

"Wait...hold up," Rhonda said and then she got quiet.

So I waited a second and then I said, "Hello," but she didn't
respond. So I said, "Rhonda, you there?"

"Girl, I'm sorry. But I had to put the phone down because
I heard a car pull up to the house."

"Is it Tony?"

"Yeah. It's him. He's out there parking his car now."

"Well, go ahead and get your thoughts together. Because
he's going to come at you with some game. But don't fall for it.
Okay?"

"Okay."

"A'ight. Well, keep your head up! And I want you to know
that I love you, girl. You have always been like a sister to me.
So I'm going to have your back, regardless of what you decide
to do. Okay?"

"Thanks, girl. And I love you, too."

Later on that night, my baby Mark sat in the living room and waited for me to get dressed so we could go to the bowling alley. Nikki and Syncere had already called and told us that they was gon' meet us at the place, so Mark put the pressure on me because he was ready to go.

"Are you ready yet?" he asked in an impatient manner.

"I'm almost," I said as I began to tie up my sneaker laces.

Immediately after, I stood up and got a glimpse of my 36-24-38 frame, and wondered how in the hell I got my big butt in these tight-ass jean shorts. And then I realized that it didn't matter because I was looking so good in them. Plus, I knew Mark was going to love it. So as soon as I grabbed my hand-bag, I cut the light out in my bedroom and headed into the living room.

"Baby, I'm ready," I told him the moment I approached him.

"Goddamn! Whatcha trying to do?" he commented.

"What are you talking about?" I played dumb. But I knew he was talking about my shorts.

"Yo, you need to go and change them, 'cause there's no way I'm gon' let you go outside with that shit on. They're too tight."

"But they're Apple Bottoms. That's how they're supposed to fit."

"Look, Kira, I ain't trying to hear that. So go and take that shit off."

"A'ight," I said and left the living room to change into some-thing a little more loose fitting, which only took me about five minutes to do. When I returned he was already standing up and waiting by the front door.

"Now that looks better," he commented the moment he laid eyes on me.

"Oh boy, hush," I replied and then I flipped the light switch off while he opened up the front door.

When we got outside, he walked ahead of me so he could unlock the passenger side door. Yeah, that's just the gentleman working inside of him. And as soon as he closed the door behind me, two guys with black masks on and guns in hand came up from behind him and started unloading their clips on us.

I heard Mark fall to the ground instantly and when I heard the loud thump, I knew in my heart that he wasn't going to be getting back up, which is why I screamed at the top of my lungs and tried to scramble to the driver's side of the car, but it was too late. I got hit with two bullets.

I felt the first one go through my right arm like a flash of lighting while the second went through my right back side.

Oh, my God! I'm getting ready to die. These bullets are burning my insides up and I'm bleeding everywhere. I need some help. But I can't move.

"Yeah, nigga! You thought it was over, didn't you? Trying to play gangsta in front of your punk ass click," I heard one of the guys yell. "Now, look at 'cha bitch ass!"

I lay there motionless. I wanted these guys to think that I was already gone.

"Take that nigga's jewels," I heard the other voice say.

"A'ight," said the first guy.

And then I heard a whole bunch of movement and commotion on the ground. It sounded like one of the guys was struggling to move Mark's body.

And as bad as it sounds, I couldn't bring myself to cry. I

was in too much pain. And not only that, I knew that if I continued to play dead, then I would stay alive.

"A'ight. Let's go," one guy said.

"Wait! Let me see if his girls still breathing."

"Yo, I stuck her first! I know she's sleeping. Now come on before the police comes."

"A'ight," the other guy replied and then I heard them both run off. About a minute later, I heard a car's tires squeal as they sped off.

Now it took every ounce of strength I had within myself to move my body. And when I was able to do this, I grabbed my cell phone out of my pocket book and dialed 911.

"911, what's your emergency," the lady said but my mouth wouldn't move. And then I went out cold and lost all consciousness.

I began to hear voices and that's when I realized that I had regained consciousness. I opened my eyes but was instantly blinded by the lights that were blaring at me from above. I closed my eyes and tried desperately to control my breathing through these plastic tubes I had plugged deep into my nose.

"She just opened and closed her eyes," I heard a familiar voice say. When I reopened my eyes once again to get a look at the person behind the voice, I managed to escape the light blaring down at me as the person who had spoken was blocking it.

"Hey look! She opened up her eyes again," the same voice commented.

Now I knew who this person was, but I wanted to make sure, so I blinked my eyes into focus and that's when I got a clear view of my cousin, Nikki.

My home girl Rhonda was also in this picture. She was standing right next to Nikki.

"Kira, baby, can you hear us?" Rhonda asked while I noticed that she had been crying.

Now it took me a minute or two, but I answered her by nodding my head "yes."

Then she asked me, "Well, can you talk?"

So I took a deep breath and began moving my lips, so the words, "Where am I?" spilled from my mouth.

"You're in the hospital," Nikki said.

"Where's Mark? Is he all right?" I asked.

But from Nikki's facial expression, I could tell that he wasn't, which wasn't good enough because I wanted answers. So I asked her again.

"Where's Mark? Is he all right?"

"He didn't make it Kira," Rhonda said. "The paramedics pronounced him dead before they could get him here. It was too late."

Hearing Rhonda's words got me choked up really bad. The lump in my throat made it very hard for me to cry out. But, it didn't stop the tears in my eyes from trickling down my face.

"No, I can't believe that," I was finally able to say.

"Listen, Kira, we couldn't believe it either. But, he's gone," Nikki stepped up and said.

"No! Nikki, you know he's a fighter."

"Kira, baby, please calm down and take it easy." Everything's going to be all right." Rhonda interjected.

"Yes, girl. Everything's gonna be all right," Nikki repeated.

And instead of uttering another word, I closed my teary eyes and just lay there as a lot of mixed emotions started overcoming me. And I'm talking about the feelings of knowing that a nigga I was starting to love is now gone and never coming back. But what's so really messed up about all of this is that I was with him when those masked muthafuckas murdered him.

Now how am I ever going to erase that night from my mind? I know that it's gonna be damn near impossible to do. I mean, what am I going to do now? How am I going to go on with my life knowing that I'm not going to be able to have him lay next to me ever again? And how am I going to be able to go home and not think about the fact that he got killed right outside my apartment?

And I know that there has to be some traces of his blood splattered all over my sidewalks. So what am I going to do? I can't go home and see that. I just can't go back there, ever.

CHANGING DA' GAME

Nikki and Rhonda stayed by my side in the hospital room the entire morning. They tried every trick they could muster up just so I could feel better about the situation. But nothing they did worked. And what made matters worse was when the doctor who performed my emergency surgery walked into the room.

"Hello, Kira. I'm Dr. Magno," the six feet tall, bald-headed Caucasian man said. "I'm just stopping by and checking in to see how you're coming along."

"Excuse me, Dr. Magno. But can you tell me how long is she going to have to be here?" Nikki jumped in and asked.

"Well, it all depends on her. But I will say she could be here for a minimum of two days."

"Two days?" I said with frustration.

"Yes, Kira. You're going to have to be here for at least two day, so we can monitor your vitals. Not only that, you lost a lot of blood as a result of an internal hemorrhage. And unfortunately, the hemorrhaging caused you to have a miscarriage."

"Wait a minute, doctor...I lost my baby?" I said aloud as my eyes filled up with tears, hoping my mind wouldn't register the thought.

"I'm sorry Kira, but, yes, you did. And I assure you that there was nothing that could be done to save the baby. However, I have requested that you see a family planning counselor before you're discharged from the hospital. So if you should have any questions, please feel free to address them to her. But in the meantime, I want you to relax yourself as much as possible. And when you start to feel the pain coming on, let your nurse know so she can give you the medicine I've prescribed for you."

"Well, doctor, can you tell us how long she's gonna have to wear those tubes in her nose?" Nikki wanted to know.

"It won't be much longer," he began saying. "Her nurse will remove them before her shift ends, which is around 3:30 this afternoon."

"Well, what about this IV? Will the nurse be taking that out too?" Rhonda jumped in and asked.

"No, we're going to leave that in for another day. And the reason for that is because we're using it to dispense her meds. Plus, she was severely dehydrated. So we have to replenish her body with the fluids needed."

"So they're going to remove it tomorrow?" Rhonda asked.

"Yes. That's exactly when it will be removed," Dr. Magno assured her.

He talked to us for a few more minutes and answered a couple more questions until he was paged over the intercom. But before he left, he assured me that he'd be back to check on me before I left the hospital for good.

Right after his departure, both Nikki and Rhonda turned back around towards me. But Nikki was the one who spoke first.

"Kira, I am so sorry about the baby," she told me as she

reached down to hug me.

"Yeah, girl, I'm sorry too," Rhonda interjected as she grabbed a hold of my hand.

"Oh, but it's going to be all right, because Syncere done already said that he's going to take care of the niggas who did this to y'all."

"Look, Nikki, I don't need that heat," I told her and when I said it, it seemed like I was talking in slow motion.

"I know you don't, Kira. But it's out of my hands."

"Okay, it's out of your hands now. But what you think them niggas gon' do to me after they find out I'm still alive?"

"Yeah, Nikki, that's a good question," Rhonda said.

"They ain't gon' do nothing to you," Nikki began explaining. "Cause as soon as you get out of here, you're coming to my house until all of this shit blows over."

"And how long do you think it's going to take for that to happen? I mean, I do want to go on with my life," I asked her because I needed some answers.

"Hopefully soon," was all she could tell me because she didn't have the slightest clue nor did she know how serious this shit was going to get. She's green as hell when it comes to the streets. So why the hell is she standing 'round here like she's a trooper suited up and ready to go to war? But it's all good, I guess.

"Does Syncere know who shot us?" I asked Nikki.

"Well, after I told him the comments you said the guys made when they were taking Mark's jewelry, he said 'a'ight' in a way like he knew who to go to."

"But, you're not sure?"

"Come on, Kira, you know a nigga like him ain't going to come out and tell his girlfriend who he's planning to get killed. All he said was that those niggas are going to pay. And that's it."

"Well, I don't want to know shit!" Rhonda interjected. "I've got enough problems of my own already."

Listening to Rhonda's comment made me realize that she's right. Who wants to know what's about to happen to those bastards that shot me and killed Mark? And as bad as I want to know who they are for my own safety, I'm just going to do the next best thing and that means remove myself from that scene. It would be the easiest method to get out of harm's way. I mean, I've already lost Mark, and then my baby. So the only other person left to go would be me. But I'm not ready to leave. I've got a lot of shit on this earth to do. And when I do it, I'm going to do it for my baby and Mark both.

"Want some more water?" Rhonda asked me.

"No, I'm okay," I told her and then I closed my eyes so I could reflect on my life and what's about to come.

The next morning two Virginia Beach homicide detectives stopped by my room to ask me some questions. However, I really didn't have the answers they were looking for, so the visit with them didn't last long at all. They did leave me their cards for just-in-case purposes.

Now my visit from Nikki didn't come until later around 5 p.m. Before she graced me with her presence, I got a surprise phone call from Ricky and some anonymous person, allowing him to use the anonymous person's three-way. And fortunately for that person, he remained quiet the entire conversation.

"Hey, I just heard about what happened. Are you a'ight?" Ricky asked in a concerned manner.

"No, I'm not. But I will be," I assured him.

"So, what is the doctor saying?"

"He said that I'm going to be all right if I relaxed and took it easy. But I did lose a lot of blood."

"So when is he letting you get out of there?"

"Between today and tomorrow."

"Who was that nigga you was with when them cats rolled up on y'all?"

"His name was Mark. Why?"

"I'm just asking, that's all."

"Well, what's the next question? Was I fucking him?"

"Were you?"

"Yeah, I was," I boldly said. And I thought Ricky was going to go off on me, but he didn't.

"Well, then, I'm sorry 'bout your loss."

"Yeah, whatever," I said, 'cause I know he was just putting on an act.

"Did the police come up there and talk to you?"

"Yeah. They just left."

"So, what they say?"

"They didn't say shit. All they wanted to know was how everything happened. So I told them what I could."

"Did you tell them who did it?"

"No."

"Why not?"

"Because I don't know," I began to explain. "They were wearing masks, so I didn't see their faces."

"You know I heard that nigga was robbing cats and that's why he got smoked."

"Who told you that dumb ass shit? 'Cause whoever said it don't know shit about him!"

"And you do?"

"Yes, I do. So don't call me with that mess."

"Look, all I'm doing is telling you what I heard from a couple of niggas in here."

"Well, them niggas in there don't know what the hell they talking about."

"So, do you know why they ran up on y'all?"

"No, I don't. But I do know that it wasn't about him robbing somebody."

"Well, what is his people's saying?"

"I don't know because I haven't talked to anybody," I lied.

"So ain't nobody been up there to holler at you?"

"No."

"Goddamn! What kind of peoples was that nigga fucking with? Shit, for all you know, them niggas could've gotten him popped," Ricky commented, but I didn't feed into his shenanigans. I know he's trying to pull information out of me. But I ain't biting. So I ignored his question. And when he realized what I was doing, he said, "Ay, Kira, you a'ight?"

"No. I'm not all right. So stop asking me that."

"Well, what are they feeding you in there?"

"They been giving me chicken broth."

"So, who gon' pick you up when it's time for you to leave?"

"Rhonda is. Why?"

"I just asked."

"Well, who's gon' pick you up when it's time for you to leave?" I came back on him. Because I know he was waiting on me to say Nikki's name, which would have made his skin crawl. But I played it safe and used somebody else's name who was also close to me.

"Hopefully you," he finally replied, catching on to my sarcasm.

"Nah, brother, you better get one of your hoes to do that."

"Did you get with my lawyer, so y'all can go and see them people for me?" he asked, ignoring my comment.

"No, I haven't seen those people yet. But I talked to your lawyer a couple of days ago about getting together with them in the next day or so. But since this mess has happened, I don't think I'm gon' be up for that."

"But you have to," Ricky said desperately. "The clock is still ticking."

"Look, Ricky, I just got shot twice, if you haven't heard. And right now, I'm laying in the damn hospital. Now I know the clock is ticking because you're reminding me of it every time I talk to you. But at this very moment, it's all about me and my health. So that bullshit you talking about is gon' have to wait until after I recover."

"Okay, hold up. I understand about all that. But the deal is on the table now. So if we drag our feet with this thing, they gon' snatch it away from me."

"That's not my problem, Ricky."

"Oh yes the fuck it is! Remember, I'm in this hellhole because of you and your big-mouth-ass cousin."

"Nah, nigga, you're in there for them murder hits. So stop trying to blame everyone else for your fuck-ups. Everybody knows what type of nigga you are. Even I know it. That's why I'm gon' look out for myself first. Fuck all that other shit you talking about."

"Well, just remember what I said is gon' happen if you try to front on me."

"Ricky, I don't care about your little threats. They don't scare me. Right now, you're talking to a chick who could care less about what happens. Shit, I just got shot and almost came close to dying. So what could you possibly do to me?"

"Put you out of your misery," he so coldly said.

"Well, then, do it, you piece of shit! Acting like you a gangsta or something. You ain't shit!"

"Oh, I'ma show you."

"Well, good, soldier. And now you ain't got to call me no more. 'Cause if you do, I'm going to get all the numbers you used to call me from, blocked."

"Fuck you! You gold-digging bitch! I'm gon' have your muthafucking head, you hoe! So you better watch your back when you leave the hospital, 'cause I'ma getcha!"

"Well, let me tell you this before you have somebody take me out," I began to say sarcastically, "I just want you to know that while you was fucking Sunshine behind my back, I was fucking your home boy Russ."

"You what!?" Ricky yelled at the top of his lungs.

"Yeah, nigga. I was fucking your big-dick friend right in our bed, when you used to leave me to go out of town."

"Yo, you're a nasty hoe! And you talking like that shit is cute," he yelled once again.

"Don't get mad 'cause his dick is bigger and better than yours. And as a matter of fact, because his dick was so good, he knocked me up with it."

"He did what?" Ricky screamed.

"You heard me, nigga."

"Nah, I ain't hear ya'. So tell me again."

"I said, he knocked me up," I repeated. "I'm pregnant with his baby and I'm going to have it, too," I lied, using this ammunition to fuel his anger.

"Oh bitch, you ain't keeping that! I can promise you that."

"And what you gon' do?"

"You'll see."

"Shut the fuck up! 'Cause you ain't gon' do a damn thing but keep running your mouth. And you gon' do that with somebody else because I'm about to hang up on your clown ass. And if you try to call this phone back, you ain't going to get through, 'cause as soon as I hang up on you I'm going to take the phone right back off the hook, so it's going to be busy."

"I ain't gon' call your trifling ass back. I'm gon' get close to you another way..." Ricky said, and before he could get another word in, I gave him the dial tone.

Now as upset as he had just got me, I couldn't believe that it didn't make me cry. I honestly didn't harbor any feelings of hurt. My heart felt so empty and cold. And right now, nothing would better soothe me than some get back. Yeah, I want to jump on the fast track to revenge. I want to see that bastard suffer really badly. And since Russ is number one on my list of niggas to get, Ricky has now just been added. So now he better watch his back. But for now, I guess I'm gon' have to settle for the fact that he's going to rot in prison for the rest of his fucked-up life because I'll die first before I help him rat Papi out! It's just not going to happen.

BACK AT THE JAIL

"Ay yo, Bossman," I called out to him when I saw him sitting at one of the card tables in the corner of the cell block by himself.

"What's good, dawg?" he replied and then stood up to give me the proper hand shake.

When he sat back down, I took a seat on the bench in front of him and said, "I need a job done."

"Whatcha need?" Bossman asked.

"I need somebody clipped."

"When you want it done?"

"As soon as possible."

"Who you want popped?"

"My wife."

"Goddamn, dawg! Your wife! What's up with that?" Bossman asked me and then he laughed.

"Yo dawg, that bitch just told me that she fucked my right hand man in our bed when I was gone out of town. And now she's pregnant by him and she's gon' keep it."

"Nah, man, she ain't told you no shit like that."

"Yes, she did. And when she was telling me that garbage, she started laughing like the shit was funny."

"Yo man," Bossman said as he shook his head in disbelief. "If my girl was to ever come out her mouth to tell me some shit like that, I'll probably be banging one of these niggas heads up against the bars in here."

"You know what, man? The way shit is ringing in my mind right now, I'm real close to doing something like that. But it ain't these nigga's heads in here that I want. It's that hoe and that tadpole in her fucking stomach."

"Yo Ricky, I'm telling you right now, my peoples gon' charge you double 'cause she's pregnant."

"Man, I don't care about that. Money is not an issue with me. But that hoe is, especially if she's still breathing past 72 hours."

"Well, if you're trying to get her done before then, then my peoples ain't gon' be able to help. They gon' need at least a week if you want shit done proper."

"What's today?"

"Tuesday."

"So, you saying your peoples can have her taken care of by Sunday?" I asked because I wanted assurance.

"Most def."

"So, what's the fee?"

"Ten grand."

"Goddamn, nigga! Whatcha trying to do to me?" I said with frustration. "I know you can do me a little better that that! So sho' me some love."

"C'mon, dawg. You know that's the going rate."

"Yeah. But, me and you peoples, though."

"A'ight listen," Bossman said, as he scratched his head, "If you can get me seventy-five large, I'll make the call."

"A'ight. Let's do it," I told him and nodded my head, 'cause I know it's a done deal. And I also know shit is gon' go nice and smooth. I just wish I could be out there to see that hoe squirming like a fucking snake when they put a slug in her head. Boy, would that make my day.

"So, when you think you can get me that dough?" Bossman asked.

"By tomorrow night."

"Good. So let me get on the horn and let my man Ty know something is about to come through. And then, after the dough changes hands, he gon' get his crew suited up. So now all you got to do is tell me where she lives at."

"Nah. That won't be a good idea."

"Why?"

"Because her house is kind of hot right now from that nigga named Mark who got killed outside her front door."

"So, where you want her done at?"

"She's in the hospital now. So have one of your boys follow her and do it then."

"When is she getting out?"

"In a day or two."

"Well, that's not gon' happen. I told you they gon' need at least a week to scope out shit. So when they hit her, it's gon' be a wrap. Nothing more."

"A'ight! Check it out! She owns a hair salon off Newtown Road, and sometimes she stays late. So that'll be the perfect spot."

"Well, a'ight. Then it's done. So, I'ma pass all this information on and give you the word when the show is over."

"Sounds good," I assured him. And then when I got up from the bench to leave he said, "Yo dawg, that *rocket*, is blazing through here. And my plate, is almost clean. Niggas is loving it."

I acknowledged his reference to the heroin I had sent to me in jail, and how the supply is now low due to its popularity. I sat back down and said, "I know. 'Cause when Bivens pulled me out of the block last night, she told me some nigga in A-block had just OD'd right before her shift started."

"Yeah, I heard some of the cats in here talking about it. They said that nigga's eye rolled to the back of his head."

"That shit must've bust his heart wide open."

"That's what I said when I heard them talking about it."

"Yo! If that shit keeps popping them like that, it ain't gon' be nobody left in this joint to make money from."

Bossman laughed at my comment, so I said, "We might have to turn the volume down on that piece."

"Nah, man. Leave it just like it is."

"Yo dawg, you must be trying to wear a couple of murder beefs. 'Cause if we don't put a lid on this shit, mu'fucka's gon' be 'round here telling them crackers where they got it from."

"Nah. It ain't gon' get that bad," Bossman said, trying to convince me. But I wasn't buying that shit, for real. I know what the consequences gon' be if niggas keep falling out 'round here.

And this nigga right here knows it too. But he don't care. All he cares about is all that dough we coming off with. But since I'm the *HNIC,* the Head Nigga In Charge, I'm gon' have to dilute it. And that's just how it's gon' be.

PIECES OF THE PIE

Nikki was here bright and early to scoop me up from the hospital. And trust me, I was ready to go. Now Syncere was waiting on us to come outside, so he could drive us back to Nikki's apartment. After he and the nurse helped me into the front seat of his truck, Nikki hopped in the back and we were off.

From the back seat Nikki started switching the radio stations with the wireless remote. But Syncere wasn't in the mood for any music. He wanted to talk about the night of the shooting.

"Nikki told me the police came by the hospital to talk to you."

"Yeah," I said, nodding my head.

"So, what were they talking about?" he continued.

"They just wanted me to tell them what I saw. So I did."

"Did you tell them what them niggas said?"

"Yeah."

"And what did they say?"

"They didn't say anything. All they did was write every-thing I said down on their little notepad."

"Well, did they say who might've shot y'all?"

"No. They seemed like they was as clueless as I was."

"Did they show you some pictures or throw any names around?"

"Nope," I said nonchalantly.

"Well, did they say they were gonna get back in touch with you, so y'all can talk again?"

"Yeah. They said they was going to call me in a few days. And they gave me their cards, too, just in case I think of some-thing that I didn't tell 'em." I switched up the conversation asking him, "Do you know who shot us?"

"No. But I'm about to find out."

"Well, do you have an idea? I mean, did Mark have beef with somebody? Or owed a nigga some money or something?"

"Nah. It wasn't none of that."

"Well, was he a stick-up kid?"

Syncere looked at me like I was losing my damn mind and said, "Kira, please don't ever disrespect me or my man by ask-ing me something like that," he began saying, "It's not that type of party with us. Ain't none of the cats in my crew cow-boys or Indians. We are legit businessmen and that's it."

"Oh, I'm sorry."

"It's okay. Everything's all love. That's why I'm putting you up at Nikki's crib. So you ain't got to worry about noth-ing."

"Yeah, girl, Syncere filled up my refrigerator with a whole bunch of groceries. He even got us some brand new DVDs to watch and we got spending money just in case we want to or-der out."

"Ahh...that was nice," I said, being phony as hell. I mean come on...what this nigga think, I'm some kind of Reebok chick?

Shit, I can cop my own self some groceries and a couple of DVDs. But what he can do is hit me off with some pain and suffering money. 'Cause I could definitely use it.

"Yes, girl," Nikki interjected, "That's my boo!"

"I know that's right," I replied, disgusted as all get out and then I turned my head to look out the window.

"Mark's funeral is this Friday," Syncere spoke again.

"It is?" I turned my focus back into his direction.

"Yeah. So do you want to go?"

"Of course. But where is it going to be?"

"Some church his moms belong to back in New Jersey."

"What time?"

"She told me it's going to start at two o'clock."

"So, what time you planning on leaving here?"

"I'ma leave VA about 6 o'clock in the morning, so I can get an early start on that heavy traffic we're going to run into."

"A'ight. Well, I'll be ready," I told him. And then I called out to Nikki and said, "Nikki, are you going, too?"

"Yep. I'm going."

"Good. I'm glad. 'Cause I'm gon' sho' need you by my side with this one."

"Trust me, I'm going to be with you every step of the way," she assured me.

Arriving at Nikki's apartment is when I realized that we had reached our final destination. Inside, Nikki had everything arranged for me. Her guest room was equipped with everything I could possibly need. Shit, I am not going to have to get up for nothing. So I'm down for that. But what I ain't down for is how Syncere tried to carry me. I mean, does he have the slightest idea of who the hell I am? 'Cause, if he doesn't, then I need to bring him up to speed about who my husband is and about how much property and dough we used to have before all that shit went down. He also needs to know that I'm the one who's feeling disrespected, not him. So when I get my chance, I will shed some light on this situation.

Meanwhile, as I was going through my emotional roller coaster, Nikki was sending Syncere on his way. After he left, she found her way back to see me in the guest room.

"You all right?" she asked me, smiling.

"I will be after this medicine starts kicking in," I said as I laid my head back in the pillow.

"Well look, I want to tell you something. But before I tell you, you've got to promise me that you won't tell anyone."

"Okay. I promise," I agreed because Nikki seemed like she was serious about this one.

"You can't tell the police, either."

"Wait!" I said as the speed of my heart started picking up. "Does this have something to do with me and Mark?"

Nikki nodded her head .

"And you don't want me to tell the police?" I asked, becoming furious with the thought.

"No. You can't. So do you promise me you won't say anything? And what I'm about to tell you won't leave this room?"

Now as bad as I wanted to tell her that I couldn't promise her that I wouldn't keep my mouth closed, I somehow knew in the back of my mind that she would refuse to tell me what was going on. So I forced myself to agree to her terms.

"Okay. Anything you hear will not leave this room. You promise?"

"Yes, I promise," I assured her.

Nikki sat down on the bed next to me and said, "When me and Syncere were asleep last night, he got a phone call on his cell phone about 11:30 p.m. So when he got out of the bed and went out on my patio, I thought that he was trying to be considerate. But then it dawned on me that since he's been acting kind of funny lately, that it could be some hoe he was fucking with behind my back. So I got out of the bed and tip-toed my butt right on over to the patio doors and stood still, so I could eavesdrop on his conversation. And lucky for me, the door was cracked a little, because if it wasn't, I would not have heard a thing."

"So, what was he saying?"

"Well, whoever he was talking to, he asked them why it took them so long to call him back? And then he said the chick that was with him that night ain't dead. So right then, I knew he was talking about you."

"What?" I said because I was getting a little confused.

"Wait! Let me finish," Nikki said.

"Go ahead," I insisted.

"Okay. And then he told the person on the phone that you heard them talking, which wasn't a good thing. But he's glad that they didn't say much."

"And why the fuck wasn't that a good thing?" I interjected. "What is Syncere—an accomplice to Mark's murder or something? Because this shit ain't adding up. I mean, why would he tell somebody that I heard the guys who shot us talking to each other, and say that it's not a good thing? It seems like he's trying to help whoever shot us cover their tracks. And I don't like that a bit. Plus, it's starting to give me the creeps. I mean, if he did have something to do with it, then what was the motive behind it? Because the last time I checked, I thought that him and Mark were homeboys?"

"I thought so, too. But after hearing this conversation, I quickly came to the conclusion that something ain't right at all."

"You damn right! So what are we going to do about it?"

"We ain't going to do nothing. Because first of all, we do not know who Syncere was talking to on his cell phone. And two, we have absolutely no proof to link him to what happened that night."

"Look Nikki," I began to say, "I can't stay here knowing all of this. And it's going to be real hard for me not to look at that nigga funny when he comes here."

"Kira, I understand that. But we cannot let on that we know what's going on."

"Well, I don't think that I'm going to be able to pull it off. So you might as well take me home."

"No, I can't let you," Nikki began saying, "Because what if those guys who killed Mark come back and try to take you out?"

"Well, after that shit you just told me, my apartment might be safer than yours."

"Listen," Nikki said, "the best thing for us to do is stick together and wait this thing out. And if Syncere did have something to do with Mark getting killed, then it'll come out. And when it does, then you and I will not have a choice about whether or not to go to the police, because we will."

I sighed heavily and said, "I am so tried of going to the police."

"I know. Me too. But somebody's got to protect us."

"Don't remind me," I told her and then I covered my entire face with the bedspread, as a gazillion thoughts began to run through my mind.

Nikki got up from the bed and said, "Go ahead and get some rest. But let me know when you need me to do something for you, okay?"

"All right."

The morning of the trip to New Jersey is when I decided that I wasn't going. Coming face to face with Mark's lifeless body is not how I want to remember him. Not to mention the thought of riding with the man who I feel had something to do with my incident and Mark's murder. Shit! It would not surprise me if this nigga's purpose for this trip is to kidnap me and Nikki and do away with our asses. So I tell you what, if it is my time to go, it will not be on a road trip. I can promise you that one.

So when Syncere finally came through, it was a little after 6 a.m. And when he saw that Nikki and I weren't dressed and still in bed, he got somewhat testy.

"Why ain't ya'll ready?" I heard him yelling from Nikki's bedroom.

"Because we're not going," she told him.

"So why didn't you call and tell me that before I took this long-ass ride over here?"

"I did. But your voicemail kept coming on the first ring."

"And when was this?"

"It was last night."

"What time?"

"I don't remember. But I did call you twice."

"That's it?"

"Yeah. I mean, what else do you want me to say?"

"Just tell me, why all of a sudden y'all changed y'all mind?"

"Well, because Kira's still in a lot of pain, so she's not in the mood for a bumpy ride."

"You sho' it's nothing else?"

"Yeah, I'm sure. I mean, what else could it be?" I heard Nikki say.

"Yo, whatever, man!" he replied and then I heard him storm out of the apartment.

Now almost immediately after Syncere vacated the premises, I heard Nikki running down the hallway in my direction.

"Hey, Kira, you up?" she asked me the instant she opened the bedroom door and poked her head in the room.

"Yeah. I'm up," I told her.

"Did Syncere's loud mouth wake you up?"

"You know it did."

"And I take it you heard every word he uttered from his mouth, huh?"

"Every word. And I could tell that he was really pissed off, too."

"Yep. He sure was. But he'll get over it."

"Well, do you think that he bought your story about me still being in pain?"

"He didn't have a choice."

"So, I heard," I commented.

"Well, he'll be gone for the whole weekend, so I guess we'll both be at peace 'round here."

"Yes. And I'm going to love every minute of it, too."

"Well, go 'head on back to sleep, then. I'm getting ready to get right back in my bed, so I can get me some more shut eye."

"All right," I said and then Nikki closed the door.

MIXING SHIT UP

After Bossman gave me word that his peoples have been having a hard time trying to run into Kira at the salon, I went on and gave them the okay to squat outside her lil' condo. But come to find out, she ain't been staying there for almost two weeks now. Bossman told me that they gon' have to pull back for a week or so, so they won't make themselves hot and draw attention to themselves. I said, a'ight. But I stressed to him that I'm gon' still need somebody to ride through every now and then, just to check to see if her whip shows up.

He agreed to have that done. But in the meantime, I see I'm gon' have to do some footwork myself because Kira's been alive long enough. It's time for her oxygen to expire. And I'm gon' speed up the process.

Later, when Lena pulled me out of the block, I ran game on her.

"Ay, baby."

"Yeah," she answered me right after she handed me my container of food.

"I'm gon' need you to do me another favor."

"And what's that?"

"Well, I'm trying to catch up with my wife. But can't nobody seem to catch up to her. So I'm gon' need you to go by there."

"And what am I suppose to say when I see her?"

"Nothing. All I want you to do is when you see her, call this number right here and my peoples will do the rest. Oh yeah, her address is up there, too."

Lena took the piece of paper outta my hand, looked at it, and said, "And whose number does this belong to?"

"Look, you don't need to know all that," I began to tell her. "All you gotta do is go by her crib, sit outside in your car, and wait for her to come home. And then, as soon as you see her, call that number and tell the person who answers it that she's home."

"But I don't understand why I gotta do all of that."

"It ain't for you to understand. Now, can you do like I asked you?"

"I don't know, Ricky," she started saying, "I mean, I'm not into the stalking thing."

"You ain't stalking her."

"Then what do you call it?"

"Look Lena, stop with the questions, 'cause this shit I need you to do is critical."

"Well, I'm sorry, Ricky. I'm just not into that type of stuff you're asking me to do."

"I don't give a fuck what kind of shit you into," I snapped, standing up in her face. "Because you gon' do it. And that's a wrap!"

"But how can you make me sit outside your wife's place and wait for her to come home?"

"Because you're my girl and I can do that," I said with authority and then I kept right on eating my food.

"But I'm not comfortable doing that."

"Lena, you doing it! So I don't wanna hear nothing else about it!"

"Well, can I ask you a question?"

"What?!"

"Are you trying to have something bad done to her?"

"Are you trying to get involved?" I asked her with the meanest grit my face could make.

"No," she told me as her lips began to tremble.

"Well, shut the fuck up! And stop asking me twenty-one questions!"

Once I said my piece, Lena caught on very quick and I didn't have any problems with her for the rest of the night.

Right after I got my stomach straight, I made her give me some head. I didn't want any pussy tonight because I wasn't in the mood for it. And as soon as my dick exploded, I wiped my shit off and I made her take me right back to the block.

PURPLE HAZE

I am beginning to feel better and better as the days go by, so today I got Nikki to drive me to my apartment, so I could grab a few things. Plus, I wanted to gather all the mail I knew I had stacked in my mailbox.

Now when I entered into my house it was crazy because I could still smell the scent of Mark's cologne lingering in the cushions of my sofa and on the pillows on my bed. I couldn't stand it, knowing that he was gone and that my house was filled with his memories. So as soon as I grabbed a bagful of my clothes and shoes, I made my exit before I had a nervous breakdown.

I walked out of my apartment first and Nikki followed, holding my bags in her hand. And as I began to limp towards my car, I pressed the unlock button on my key ring.

"Press the trunk button, too," Nikki said as she approached the back of my car.

And then as I grabbed onto the door handle to open the passenger side door, a powder blue, late model Nissan Maxima pulled up next to my car with a Spanish-looking chick behind the steering wheel. She looked like she was lost and was about to ask me or Nikki for directions to someplace. But I was wrong.

"Are you Kira?" she asked me in a very forward manner, looking directly into my face.

"Who wants to know?" I asked because this chick was making me feel leery as hell right now.

Nikki noticed this as well because she immediately shut the trunk of my car and walked over to where this chick and I were standing.

"Yeah, who wants to know?" Nikki also said.

"My name is Lena Bivens. And I work over at the same jail where your husband Ricky is an inmate."

"Okay. I'm Kira. Now, what can I do for you?" I asked because I was very anxious to know what she was about to say.

"Well Kira, I'm just going to give it to you straight," she began saying. "For the past month I've been involved with your husband on many levels."

"Oh really? So does one of those levels consist of you fucking him?" I smiled because now I was starting to get amused.

"Yes. And I don't know how I allowed him to get me all caught up in his web, but for the last few weeks I've been bringing him food in from the streets. And just recently, I've been sneaking him drugs in off the street, so he can get his hustle on...."

"So you came way over here to tell me that?" I interjected.

"No, Kira. That's not it."

"Well, damn, he's got you doing more shit?"

"Kira, I think he's trying to have somebody hurt you."

"And what makes you say that?" I asked as I began to feel the butterflies spiraling in the pit of my stomach.

"Well, because when I pulled him out of his cell a couple nights ago, he told me that he's been having major problems with a couple of his people trying to catch you at home. So now he needs me to stake out your apartment and as soon as I see you, I'm supposed to call this number right here." She held a piece of paper in her hand for me to grab. I took it out of her hand frantically and said, "And who does this number belong to?"

"I don't know."

"So, you're telling me that you're supposed to call this number without asking for someone by name?"

"Yep. That's exactly what I was instructed to do. As a matter of fact, I asked him who was I suppose to ask for and he told me nobody."

"What!" I commented with uncertainty.

"Yes. He told me that whoever answered the phone, just say the words, *she's home*. And then they would take care of the rest."

"Oh, my God! This nigga is trying to have me killed for real!" I said in a somewhat frantic way.

Nikki pulled me into her arms and said, "That bastard is crazy! So come on and let me get you out of here."

"Yeah, get her out of here. Because for all we know, he could have somebody watching me talking to y'all right now."

"We wouldn't put it past him," Nikki commented as she took a brief look around our immediate surroundings and then brought her attention back to me, to help me get into the car. "But I hope you're learning something from this," Nikki continued. "Because sooner or later, he's going to turn on you and do the same thing he's doing to her, to you. So you better get as far away from him as soon as you can."

"Trust me, I've already seen it coming. When I told him I wasn't up for watching Kira's place, he threatened me. So that's when I called it quits and put in my transfer papers. But before I bailed out of there, I felt it was my duty to let you know what he was trying to do."

"Thanks, Lena. I mean, you have no idea what you've just done for me."

"She just saved your life. That's what she's done," Nikki interjected.

"Don't thank me. Just get your butt out of here."

"You ain't got to tell her twice," Nikki spoke out once again as she got into the driver seat of my car.

"Be safe," Lena told us.

"We will. And thanks again," I told her and then she drove off.

Nikki pulled off right behind her, but made a detour at the next block.

"Can you believe that shit we just heard?" she asked me.

"Girl, nothing Ricky does surprises me anymore."

"But did you get a good look at home girl?"

"Yeah, I saw her. She's definitely his type of woman. That's why I believe everything she said. I just can't stop thinking about how fast he got her to give him some pussy."

"He sho' knows how to work his magic, huh?"

"Oh yeah, he's definitely a wiz when it comes to that type of shit! But what's getting me is the fact that he's going out of his way to get one of his people's to knock me off."

"But why, though?" Nikki wondered out loud.

I didn't want to tell her about the deal he tried to set up with me because then she would know that her head was also on the line. But now I figure that it was too late for that.

"Because I won't help him get out of jail," I finally said.

"Get out of jail, how?"

"Listen Nikki, Ricky knows about all the information you and I gave to the Feds to have him indicted."

"You're lying!" she commented with a frightened expression on her face.

"No, I'm not."

"So how did he find out about this?"

"Well, this chick who's friends with his baby's mama Frances told her that she saw me coming out of the FBI building right before Ricky got arrested. So ol' big mouth waited around for Ricky to call her and that's when she spilled the beans."

"So, how did I come into the picture?"

"Well, because he got his lawyer to check Frances' story. And when he did, that's when he found out about you and the information you gave, too."

"So does he have a hit out on me, too?" Nikki asked me as the pitch of her voice turned up.

"If he did, don't cha think that chick Lena would've mentioned it?"

"Well, tell me how you were supposed to help him get out of jail."

"Nikki," I said and then I sighed heavily, "Ricky wants me to help a couple of Feds set up a buy for a couple of bricks from this Spanish guy named Papi, so they can bust him. And then after that happens, he can get his prison sentence reduced significantly. But I refused to do it. So he told me over the phone that he's going to have my head."

"Damn! That nigga is crazy!"

"You're telling me!" I replied sarcastically.

"So who's this Papi cat?"

"He's a rich-ass, older guy from Costa Rica. But he's been living in D.C. for about fifteen years and owns a couple of stores out there, too. Ricky has been knowing him since he was about sixteen. As a matter of fact, Papi took Ricky under his wing, showed him the ropes and gave him his first package. And from there, Ricky has always looked at Papi as being like a father to him."

"Well, I wonder what Papi would say if he found out that his fake-ass son is trying to build a Fed case against him?"

"I don't know," I began to say as an idea popped into my mind. "But I will find out," I continued, pulling my cell phone from out of my hand bag.

"What are you going to do?"

"I'm gonna call Papi and let him know that I'm going to be taking a trip up to D.C. to see him," I said, searching for his phone number through the list of numbers I had programmed in my phone.

"But you're not in any shape to drive that distance."

"I know. That's why you're going with me," I continued, and then I pressed the talk button.

"But..." she tried to say.

I interjected by saying, "Shhhhhh..." because by this time, Papi had picked up his line.

"*Hola*," he said.

"Hi, Papi." I replied.

"Who is this?"

"This is Kira. Ricky's wife."

"Oh, hi love. How are you?"

"I'm okay. But I could be doing a lot better."

"Well, where have you been? I thought you were going to come out and see me."

"I was. But something came up."

"Is there any way I can help?"

"Well, yeah. But I would like to come by and talk to you about it in person, if that's all right."

"Oh, yeah. That's fine. So when are you coming by?"

"In the morning."

"Okay. Well, I guess I'll see you then."

"All right. Thanks."

"No problem, baby. Now drive safe."

"I will," I assured him.

TAKING IT TO DA STREETS

It's only been about six months since I last saw Papi, with his shiny bald head and silver-colored beard. But I must say that he ages pretty damn fast. And he's put on a lot of weight, too, with his stomach poking out, looking like he's nine months pregnant. It's probably all those plates of stew chicken and red beans and rice that's blowing him up. But hey, if he likes it, I love it. So as I walked slowly towards him, he stood up from the chair by the register and said, "Welcome, mamí!" And then he kissed me on both sides of my cheeks and embraced me with one of the tightest hugs he could muster up.

I hugged him back and said, "Thanks for having me."

"Here, have a seat," he insisted as he pulled out a chair from a nearby table.

As soon as I sat down he yelled out the name Sara, who had to be the pretty, young looking woman watching TV over by the glass refrigerator that stored the cold drinks. She was the only other person in the store. When she finally responded, he said, "Get Kira a cold soda."

"No. I'm fine," I told them both.

"Are you sure?" he wanted to know.

"Yes, Papi. I am sure."

"Okay. So, tell me what you want to talk to me about."

Before I opened my mouth to utter a word, I pulled my blouse up high above my gunshot wounds so he could take a glimpse of them.

"You see this?" I finally said as my eyes began to fill up with tears.

"What happened?" he asked me as he got a closer look.

"A couple of guys ran up on me and shot me a few weeks ago."

"Well, I see that. But who did it?"

"Ricky had a couple of his peoples from the streets to do it," I lied and said.

Now, I did this because I needed something to back up the true part of the story I was about to tell him.

"But why would he get someone to shoot you?" he began to ask. "Are you cheating on him?"

"No, Papi. I'm not. Remember when I called you a few weeks ago, with Ricky on three-way?"

"Yeah."

"And remember when he said he wanted to make a big hit so he can come up with some money to give to his lawyer?"

"Yeah."

"Well, that was a lie. Because we don't have that type of money he was talking about laying around. The Feds took everything we had, which is why he's working with them."

"Wait! You said he's working with them?"

"Yes, Papi. And he's trying to set you up, too."

"Set me up!" Papi said in a baffled kind of way.

"Yeah. That life sentence he's got is starting to weigh him down. So he wants out. And the only way to do it is to help the

Feds bring somebody like you down with him."

"Oh, really?"

"Yes, really. And he told me that if I didn't help him carry this thing out, then he was going to have my head, which is why I'm like this."

This time Papi didn't speak nor respond to the words I had just spoken. I'm guessing he's probably bugging out in his mind right now. I continued by saying, "Now, I know what I'm saying to you is kind of a hard pill to swallow. But I would not have come all the way up here if it wasn't true. Ricky is grasping for straws, Mr. Papi. And when he ran his whole scheme down to me, he told me that the Feds were going to provide me with the money and a wire to wear. So I flat out told him no and that he was wrong for trying to do this to you, because of the history y'all had and all the years that you've been good to him."

"And what did he say?"

"He said, 'fuck you!' And that it's every man for himself."

"Oh, he did?" Papi commented like he was truly appalled.

"Yes, he did."

"Well, does he know that you've come here to see me?"

"No. I didn't tell him."

"Where is he?"

"The Feds got him housed in federal lock-up at the Virginia Beach City Jail."

"Do you know how long he's going to be there?"

"No. But I do know the reason why Russ didn't get Fed time like everybody else did."

"Well, tell me," Papi insisted.

"Because he was supposed to help Ricky build a case against you," I lied once again. Hey, Russ is on my shit list, too. And why not kill two birds with one stone?

"Oh, really."

"Yes. I was told by Ricky's attorney that Russ had already given them a lot of information about you, he just didn't go through with everything else. And I was told that the Feds are looking for him right now."

I continued pouring the lies on thick because at this rate, there's no question that Papi would eliminate his ass too. So, so long ex-baby daddy!

"Is that so?" Papi finally said.

"Unfortunately, that's the way it is."

He stood up from his chair, throwing both of his hands in the air and said, "After all the shit I've done for the both of them, and this is how they repay me!"

Then he picked up the chair he was sitting in and threw it across the room, which scared the hell out of me. I was ready to leave right then and there. So I stood up and said, "I'm sorry about everything, Mr. Papi. But I couldn't sit back and let you wander around in the dark about all the stuff that's going on."

"No, love!" he said, turning on his charm. "There's no need for any apologies from you. Because you did a very good deed. And that's why I'm going to reward you. So, wait right here." He walked behind a black curtain, which led to the back of the store. About one minute later, he reappeared with a package wrapped in a brown paper bag.

"Here's something for your troubles," he said, handing me the package. "Now, I want you to take a trip. Stay out of sight for a while until all of this blows over."

Now, I started not to take the package, but I figured it had to be money. But I said, *fuck it!* And took it!

"Thanks," I said.

"No problem. Now, do like I said and go away for a while."

"Don't worry! Because I'm going to do just that," I assured him. And then I kissed him on his cheek and said, "Goodbye."

The moment I stepped foot out of the store is when I felt a sense of relief. It just felt like all the weight I had piled on my shoulders had been lifted off. And knowing that Papi was going to take care of the situation put me even more at peace. So now it's time to celebrate.

When I got back into the car, Nikki was on her cell phone feeding Syncere a whole bunch of lies about where she was. Once she managed to get him off the phone, I pulled the brown paper bag from out of my purse.

"What's that?" Nikki wondered aloud as she sped off into the road.

"Money."

"How much?"

"I don't know," I replied as I unraveled the bag and then I pulled the stack of bills out.

"Goddamn!" she commented as her eyes caught a peek. "That's a lot of damn money."

"I know," I replied, agreeing with her. Then I started counting it, which didn't take long to do, because all five stacks of bills were sectioned off with labels marked with the sum of $5,000 on each. "It's $25,000," I finally said.

"It's what?" Nikki asked, like she wasn't sure about what I had just said.

"I said, it's $25,000."

"Wait! He gave you that?"

"Yep. And I didn't even ask for it."

"So, why did he give it to you?"

"He said he was giving it to me as a reward for the good deed of telling him what Ricky was trying to do to him."

"And what do you think he's going to do about it?"

"Let's just say that I'm not gonna have to worry about my life anymore."

"Did he say he was going to have Ricky killed?"

"No. But Papi has a reputation for keeping thieves and rats away from him. So it wouldn't surprise me if he did."

"Well, what are you going to do with that money?"

"Papi told me to take a trip with it and stay out of sight for a while. So I guess that's what I'm going to do."

"Well, where are you going?"

"You mean, we?" I said smiling.

"Okay. Where are we going?" she rephrased her question.

"How about the Bahamas?" I suggested.

"The Bahamas!" she replied with excitement.

"Yeah, the Bahamas."

"Are you for real?"

"Yes, I'm for real. Because it's time for us to chill out and unwind," I continued, and then I looked out of the window and began to stare at the sky, wondering what Papi was doing back at his store. I know he's gotten on the phone with at least one of his hit men by now. So I know it won't be long for Russ and Ricky's demise.

"Okay, can we stop and get something to eat?" Nikki interrupted my thoughts.

"Yeah, c'mon," I insisted.

"Where you want to go?" she asked me.

"I don't know. But take a right at this next block and let's see what we run into," I told her. So she took heed to my instructions and did just that. We rode for about two more blocks and saw a West Indian spot to our right. So we stopped.

Nikki decided to go in and get two take about orders of oxtails with rice and peas while I stayed and waited in the car. And to my surprise, it didn't take her long at all to *cop* us some food because she was in and out of the restaurant in seven minutes flat.

"Damn! That was quick!" I commented as I took the two food-filled containers out of her hand.

"That's because there wasn't nobody in there."

"Well, that's sure a red flag that their food might be garbage."

"No it's not. It's good."

"How you know?"

"Because I asked them to give me a sample."

I giggled and said, "Girl, you are so ghetto."

"Oh, nah! You ain't seen ghetto until you see me tear into my food while I'm taking us back down the road."

"We ain't got to leave right now. So relax yourself and enjoy that food, 'cause, I sure am."

"Well, since you insist," she commented stopping her words in mid-sentence to inhale the aroma of her food. "Goddamn! This shit smells good as hell!" she continued immediately after opening up the lid to the container.

"Oh yeah, this is good," I said.

"I told you," she agreed plowing a forkful of meat and rice into her mouth.

And then with the help of her peripheral vision, her attention shifted to the left side of the car. She said, "Look at this fucking Benz. Now I know that joint got to be a '06model, 'cause niggas down our way ain't even pushing one yet."

"Yeah, that's definitely a '06. And it's hot, too!" I commented as I watched the driver park the car directly in front of us.

"Check out the thirty-day plates."

"I see them," I said taking another bite of my food as we both locked eyes on this 4-door, pearl white E-Class Sedan.

Then only seconds later, a very attractive, light-skinned, nicely shaped woman with long hair hopped out of the driver side like she was mad at the world. Immediately after she slammed her door, the passenger side door opened up and fate reared it's ugly face.

"That must be her man," Nikki commented.

"It wouldn't surprise me because that's the no-good mutha'fucka' who I was pregnant by!" I replied after adjusting to the knot in my stomach.

"That's Russ?" Nikki asked me as if it was very hard for her to fathom the idea.

"Yeah. That's the bastard that ran off with all my fucking money," I said as I shoved my food near the armrest. And then I abruptly forced open the passenger side door and got out.

"Hey Kira, whatcha getting ready to do?" Nikki began to ask me, stuttering her words as she scrambled to get out of the car behind me.

But answering her question was the least of my concern. My main objective at this point was to confront this nigga once and for all. I want him to see me face to face after all this time. And I want his bitch to see me. I want her to know that for a brief time I was in his life and I was pregnant with his child. Plus, that I'm the reason why she's pushing that fucking Benz.

"Hey Kira, wait!" I heard Nikki say from behind me.

I ignored her and rushed towards Russ and this chick he

was with. They heard Nikki call out my name because they looked directly at me as I proceeded to walk in their direction.

And with only three feet in distance between us, I felt it was time for me to lash out at him with my tongue.

"I guess you thought you'd never see me again, huh?" I retorted with rage and resentment in my voice.

"Who is that?" the chick asked Russ, who tried to escape into the restaurant, but she grabbed a hold of his arm.

And since he didn't reply, I said, "I'm Kira from VA. Russ and I used to fuck around with each other until one day he decided to rob me for more than $300,000 of my money, which I'm sure he used to *cop* that Benz you pushing and that muthafucking Bentley Coupe he just got himself."

"How you know about my Bentley?" he asked.

"I know everything about you. You piece of shit!" I screamed, but this time I was within inches of him.

The young lady with him blurted out, "Wait a minute, y'all were fucking around?"

"Yes, we sho' was. And I'm pregnant with his baby right now," I couldn't help but lie.

"You're what?" she yelled.

"I'm pregnant with his baby," I repeated myself, but in a more overbearing way so that it would somehow register in his mind. I wanted some feedback from him.

Russ snatched his arm away from her and said, "Man, fuck this!" and stormed off back into the direction of the car.

"Oh, so you ain't got nothing to say?" I yelled as I followed behind him.

"Yeah Russell, you don't have anything to say?" the woman asked as she began to follow him as well.

Yet he refused to respond to either of us. So I sprinted over towards him with my fist balled up in a knot and swung at him as hard as I could. To my surprise, my fist landed on the back of his head and stung him real good.

"What the fuck!" he said as he grabbed the back of his head with his palm.

"Bitch, don't be putting your fucking hands on my man!" The chick yelled in defense of Russ.

"Yeah Kira, don't put your hands on me no more," he insisted in a way like he wants me to heed his warning.

"Fuck you, nigga! Whatcha gon' do?" I replied, getting all cocky, awaiting another opportunity to hit him again.

"Come on Kira, let's go," Nikki interjected.

"Wait!" the woman blurted out, "I want to know when was the last time you and him been together?"

"Jessica, give me the keys or unlock this door. 'Cause I ain't got time for this shit!" Russ demanded.

"Oh, so you're Jessica?" I asked after a light went off in my head.

"Yeah, why?" she asked me.

"You just had a baby, didn't you?"

"Yes," she replied with uncertainty.

"Well, congrats to you, so now I can tell my baby that he or she's going to have a playmate."

"Won't you stop with the bullshit, Kira! You know that ain't my baby!"

"Oh, this baby is yours," I replied, rubbing my stomach in a circular motion. "So get ready, baby daddy."

"How many months are you?" Jessica asked me.

"I'm three months. And so that you know, the whole time Russ was back in VA, he was sleeping in my bed damn near every night, and lying about not having a woman when he wasn't licking on my pussy!"

"That's a lie, baby! Don't believe that shit!" he snapped.

"Oh, so I'm lying, Russ?" I asked him as I began to get angrier by the minute.

"Yeah, your crazy ass is lying! And I'm wondering what Ricky would do if he heard you running your mouth out here like this?"

"Trust me, he already knows about us. And just last week, I told him about the baby."

"What Ricky?" Jessica asked Russ.

"My partner Ricky."

"You're talking about the one that just got locked up?" her questions continued.

"Yep, that's my husband," I blurted out. "And he knows that the day you fucked me at the hotel and tied me up to the bed is the very same day you robbed me for his dough," I continued.

"So what the fuck does that mean?" Russ snapped once again.

"Oh, you'll see. So don't think you're going to keep riding around in your new *whips* like you got it going on. 'Cause one of these days, you're going to want to go out and take a stroll and your brakes will be stripped. So from this day forward, dress in black!"

"Whatcha just say?" Jessica asked.

"Sorry! But I was talking to my baby daddy," I commented and then I turned my back to the both of them and started walking in the direction of my car.

"Bitch, you threatening me?" Russ screamed. "Because we can end this shit now!"

I ignored him and continued to make my way back to my car because I felt like I said what I had to say. My point was made.

And besides, I could tell from the tone of his voice that he had his *heat* nearby. My guess is that he has it under the passenger seat of her car. My best bet is to get the hell out of dodge before he decides that he wants to use me or my car for target practice. But not only that, I'm way up in DC, in his part of town. So, who's going to come running to my rescue? Nobody! Which is why I demanded Nikki follow my lead.

Almost immediately after we got back into my car, Nikki had the gear in *drive* and we were on our way.

It only took us about forty seconds to ride by Russ and Jessica. And within that brief moment, I could hear Jessica screaming her head off at Russ, who by this time was sitting back in the passenger seat of the car. So, I rolled down my window and yelled out, "Sleep with one eye open!"

Back on the highway, Nikki had a whole lot of questions for me and even though I wasn't in the mood to comment on any of them, I did it anyway.

"Are you alright?" she asked me.

"No. But I'll be fine after Papi works his magic," I assured her.

"You know what? I don't blame you. Because that nigga was back there acting like he ain't did shit to you! I mean, he was acting like you was invading in on his space."

"I know. That's why I went off like I did."

"Yeah, I saw that. But, whatcha think Russ is going to do now that he thinks Ricky knows about him robbing you?"

"I don't know. But I'll bet my life that that nigga is in deep thought right now. He knows what Ricky is capable of doing and how strong his street soldiers are. So trust me, he doesn't want to have a war with Ricky."

"Well, he might go to Papi with it."

"Nah, he ain't going to do that. Papi will be the last person he tells about the money he took from us. That'll put him in major violation and he'll get dealt with immediately."

"What's the violation?"

"Niggas from the same squad are forbidden to rob each other, much less fuck their wives. And if Papi gets wind of that, Russ knows that he'll get wasted."

"Goddamn! I would sure hate to get on Papi's bad side."

"Me too. That's why I have no regrets for doing what I did back at the store."

"Well, after seeing Russ in rare form back there, I'm glad you did," Nikki commented. "And did you see that chick Jessica, like she was going to do something?"

"Yeah. But, you see she didn't jump my way."

"Oh, that's because the hoe wasn't crazy. All she wanted were some answers."

"And that's why I tried to give her every detail."

"Well, do you think she's going to leave him?"

"Would you, after he just *copped* you a brand new Benz?"

"Hell, nah."

"Well, there's your answer," I told her.

We continued on with our conversation about Russ and Jessica for the duration of our ride home, which, of course, gave me a bad taste in my mouth. But it'll all be over soon enough.

TURNING UP
DA HEAT

It's ten o'clock in the morning and I've got some new rookie C.O. by the name of Pippens, pulling me out of cell block, talking about I gotta go to Central Booking.

"Yo man, why I gotta go to Booking?" I asked while he was handcuffing me.

"Because it's two U.S. Marshals down there waiting for you."

"For what?"

"I don't know. But I'm sure they'll tell you when you see them."

"Ay, man, well let me ask you this."

"What is it?"

"Is Bivens supposed to be working tonight?"

"Didn't you hear?" Pippens asked me.

"Hear what?"

"She doesn't work here anymore."

"When did that happen? 'Cause I just seen her about four days ago."

"Yeah, that was her last day."

"Word!" I said like I was cool with what he just said. But on a real note, I was mad as a muthafucka'! I mean, how the fuck could she run out on me? I needed her stupid ass! So who am I gon' get to bring me shit in from off the streets now?

When this rookie-ass nigga finally made it down to Booking, I was handed over to these two militant-looking losers who called themselves U.S. Marshals. Both of them were tall and stocky. They looked like two tobacco-chewing rednecks. But when they opened up their mouths to chat to me, I knew I had to paint another picture of 'em.

"You ready?" one of 'em asked me, looking all goofy and shit after he signed off on this yellow piece of paper.

"Where y'all taking me?" I asked as they started escorting me towards the garage of the jail.

"We're transferring you to another jail," the other guy said.

"What?" I said because I don't think I heard homeboy right.

"I said, we're transferring you to another jail," the same guy said.

"But why?" I began to ask because I was becoming really fucking mad at the thought of leaving this jail while I've got unfinished business here. I mean, I've got dough owed to me from all over the place. So how am I gon' get it now that I'm breaking camp? Man, I'm fucked!

"Because one of the jail officials notified us that an inmate tipped them off that another inmate was going to try and take you out."

"Yo man, you're bugging! 'Cause ain't nobody here crazy enough to try that shit! Do you know who I am?"

"Apparently they do. So here we are."

"But I can handle myself."

"Ricky, we couldn't chance it because you're government property."

"And what the fuck does that mean?"

"It means that your safety is top priority. So it's our duty to protect you."

"But I can protect myself," I told them. Because I can. I mean, I wished a muthafucka would've ran up on me, trying to pop some shit! Yeah, I would've lit his ass up! And that ain't no lie. That's my word.

"Watch your head," the other cracker told me as he helped me get in the back of an unmarked car with tinted windows. So I did what he said and then I said, "Who gon' get my stuff from outta my cell?"

"We've got another marshal who will be on his way to pick it up in another hour."

"Does my lawyer know about y'all moving me?"

"I'm not sure. But the federal agents you're working with know," said the driver as he drove out of the underground garage.

"Oh, so y'all already talked to Reynolds and Strassman?"

"Yep. Because when they found out that your life was in danger, they wasted little time in getting the witness protection paperwork over to us."

"Witness protection!" I yelled out. 'Cause these niggas are crazy. I ain't trying to be in no fucking witness protection. So I told 'em.

"Yo, partners, I ain't trying to be in no witness protection program."

"I'm sorry, but it's too late," the passenger commented.

"That's bullshit! It ain't too late."

"Yes, it is. Because once you've assisted an agent with a federal investigation, your life becomes a target. And when that target is compromised, then you're put in witness protection."

"So, you telling me that the cats I done told the Feds about is after me?"

"That's what we were told," the driver continued.

"But how did they know?" I said out loud but the thought was for my mind to figure out.

"Because your wife told him," the passenger turned around and said as he pointed a 9 millimeter semi-automatic weapon in my face with a silencer attached.

And before I could say a word, he said, "Papi, sends his regards," and pulled the trigger.

THE ANTIDOTE

I took a trip just like Papi told me to. And believe you me, I had a blast. But it seemed like my seven-day trip ended very quickly, so you know I hated to come back home. Here I am at Nikki's house, unpacking all the new shit I bought while I was away.

After everything was put away, I lay back on this guest bed I've been sleeping on for the last month and a half to get me some rest and here comes Nikki, running towards me with the cordless phone in her hand.

"Here, listen to this," she insisted as she pressed the phone against my ear.

That's when I realized that it was a voice message left by Rhonda.

"Nikki, when you get this message tell Kira to turn on her cell phone or call me back at the shop because it's all over the news that Ricky got shot in the head by two white guys who were posed as U.S. Marshals. The police found him dead in the back of a look-a-like police car. Oh yeah, tell her that two police detectives and a FBI agent came up here to talk to her yesterday after it happened. But since she wasn't here, they left their phone numbers for her to call them. So give her this message and tell her to call me, so I can give her their numbers. Okay. Talk to you soon," Rhonda added and then she ended the message.

I pulled the phone away from my ear and looked directly into Nikki's eyes. But I couldn't say anything because my mind was still trying to absorb the fact that Ricky was now dead.

A second later, I got an odd feeling that started circulating in the pit of my stomach. I mean, could you believe it? I was beginning to feel sorry for that heartless bastard. So then I had to remind myself of all the bullshit he has ever taken me through. And that's when I began to come back to my senses.

"So, Papi really did it, huh?" I commented in a nonchalant way. Now, I can go back home without looking over my shoulder every step I take.

"But, how?" Nikki asked, with a puzzling expression.

"You heard the message."

"But how were those fake cops able to sign him out of jail?"

"They must've had the proper paperwork."

"Damn! That's scary shit!"

"What?"

"To know that Papi has power like that."

"I know. And Ricky wondered why I refused to help him set Papi up. I mean, you see how easy it was to pop him. Just think how really easy it would've been to get me."

"Girl, don't even think about it. Just put all this shit behind you. 'Cause it's over now."

"Yeah, I know. But remember there's two detectives and a FBI agent that wants to talk to me."

"Let 'em talk. I mean it ain't like you killed him. And besides, if they want to know where you were at, just show them your flight tickets and hotel reservations from our trip."

"Nikki, you took those words right out of my mouth," I told her.

Then I went into strategy mode. And since I wanted to do it alone, I asked Nikki to leave me by myself for a while, because, I wanted to be ready when I finally met with these muthafuckas. And even though they can't prove that I had something to do with his murder, I am still going to be on my toes.

Against Nikki's wishes, I gathered all of my things the following morning because I was ready to go home. I was psyched to know that I was about to start my life all over again. And this time it's going to be hassle free.

After I packed everything in the trunk of my car, I got behind the driver seat and headed on home. I accomplished this because Nikki got up and left this morning before I woke up. She said she had a breakfast date with Syncere, so she would be back in a couple of hours. And when I heard that tad bit of information, I used it to my advantage.

Now when I arrived in front of my apartment building, I hesitated before I got out of my car. I did this because I could still see a few spots of Mark's blood dried up in the cracks of the pavement right in front of my door. Naturally I reflected back on what had happened the night of the shooting. And that's when I broke down in tears. I know that spot right there is going to constantly remind me of that night, which was our last night together.

And what's so crazy is that I've been busting my brain trying to figure out why he got killed, and if Syncere had something to do with it. I mean come on, Mark was a cool-ass nigga. And plus, I was beginning to really start loving him. But those two coward-ass niggas took him away from me. And now he's gone forever. This will take me some time to get over. Now I know that the best thing for me to do is to move. I've got to. This will be the only other way I will be able to go on with my life. So I guess that's the next step.

GAME OVER

Not even a second after I walked through the front door of my apartment, my cell phone started ringing. So I threw all of my things down on the floor to retrieve my phone from my handbag.

"Hello," I said.

"Hey, where you at?" Nikki asked me.

"At home. Why?" I replied and then I took a seat on my living room sofa.

"I'm on my way over there."

"Why? What's wrong?"

"Syncere did it."

"Did what?"

"I just found he's involved with Mark getting killed."

"How did you find that out?"

"Because when he was in the shower this morning, I went through his Sidekick to see if he had any text messages from any chicks, and that's when I ran across an old message he had received the same night you and Mark got shot."

"What did the text message say?" I asked as my heart

sunk into the pit of my stomach.

"It said, 'Squad leader was with his broad, so we had to plug both of them. We got his heat, jewels and his dough, so holla at me when you want me to make the drop off.'"

"Oh, my God!" I said out loud. "We gotta call the police."

"I know, but what are we going to tell 'em?"

"We gon' tell them that, that muthafucka' had my man killed," I screamed at the top of my lungs.

"But, we have no proof."

"Where's his Sidekick?"

"He has it."

"Well, it doesn't matter,' cause I'ma call the police anyway. Ain't no way I'm gon' let that bastard walk the streets as a free man after today."

"Will you wait until I get there?"

"You better hurry up."

"I am. So give me about thirty minutes. 'Cause I'm way out here in Newport News."

"Well, I'm going to jump in the shower, so you better come on."

"Okay," she replied and then we both hung up.

Here I am pissed off once again, but hurt more or less about knowing Syncere is the one who had Mark killed. So what am I going to do? How are we going to prove the allegations? We have no murder weapon nor a motive, as the police would say. Our best bet is to get that T-Mobile away from him, which will be very hard to do. But I'll figure something out. I owe him at least that.

Anyway I got undressed and hopped in the shower because my body needed it badly. The hot water piercing the tender parts of my muscles felt great, so I took my time and bathed every inch of my body.

Now when I was done, I turned off the water and flung back

the shower curtain. And there standing before me was a man pointing his gun directly at me. I wanted to scream. But before I could let out a single cry, he said, "I'm warning you, don't scream!"

"Okay," I said with my hands partially covering my mouth.

"Here, take this," the guy told me as he handed me a newspaper clipping.

So, I reached for it and grabbed it like he instructed me to. And that's when he said, "Papi wanted me to give you that. So, you can see that he took care of Russ, too."

Hearing this man tell me that this article was about Russ made me want to read it. And there it was, typed in black on the *Washington Post*'s Metro section, about an execution style murder of a Russell Hastings, who was found in his bed at one o'clock in the morning, shot in the head three times. Police have no suspects at this time.

"This is Russ?" I asked the guy.

"Yes. That's him."

"So, can I ask you why you got that gun pointed at me?

"Because, my job is not finished."

"What do you mean?" I began to stutter, trying to figure out what was this man talking about.

"I heard you talking on the phone about calling the police. And that's not good."

"But it was for something else," I began to plead.

"I heard you. And you were talking about your husband's murder."

"No. I wasn't. I swear."

"Now, why are you lying to me? When I already heard everything you said."

"Listen, it's not what you think. I promise you that I wasn't talking about my husband's murder. I could care less about that muthafucka."

"Well, it doesn't matter anyway. Because you took money from Papi."

"But I didn't ask for it. He just gave it to me."

"But you took it. And when you did that, that let him know that you're weak and you can be bought at any price. So now you got to go, too."

"But wait!" I screamed, because I wanted to explain myself. But it was too late. He had already pulled the trigger. That meant that my life as we know it was running on empty as my soul began to emerge from my body.

COMING SOON

SEX, SIN & BROOKLYN II
BY
CRYSTAL LACEY WINSLOW
FEBRUARY 2006

CROSS ROADS
BY
CARL PATTERSON
MARCH 2006

THE BEGINNING TO THE END
BY
ENDY
APRIL 2006

THE CRISS CROSS
THE SIZZLING CONCLUSION TO LIFE, LOVE & LONELINESS

THE WIFE

**IN A WORLD WHERE EVERYONE WANTS TO BE
"WIFEY" THE QUESTION IS—CAN YOU PLAY YOUR
POSITION AND HANDLE THE DRAMA THE STREETS
WILL THROW YOUR WAY?**

THE KARMA

A child of circumstance, Myra's life is full of abuse, neglect and hard knocks. Myra's life takes a dramatic turn when she earns a full scholarship. Determined and with her best friend by her side, Myra's life is finally on track. She meets Milton Roberts, convinced that he is just the man to save her from her harsh life. Until...

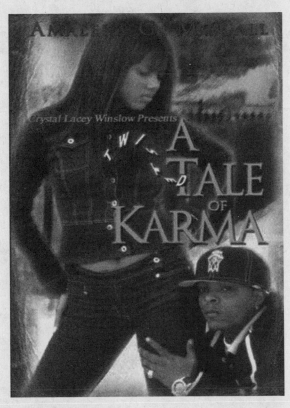

UP CLOSE & PERSONAL
A POETRY BOOK THAT READS LIKE A NOVEL!

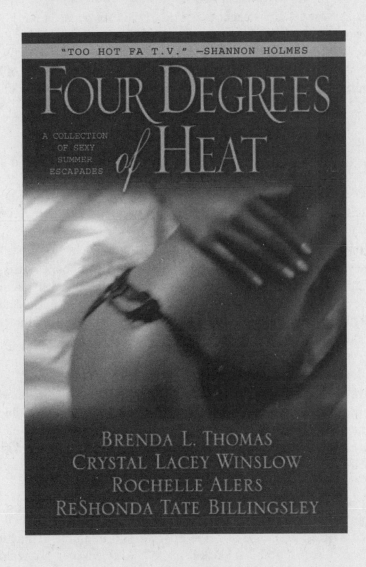

MENACE II SOCIETY
COMING SOON IN 2006

Walk With Me Al-Saadiq Banks
Newark, New Jersey is eager to get rid of the infamous, Miracle. A predicate with a long list of felonious crimes. When he's arrested for the brutal murders of his two co-defendants, he realized that his life is over. Walk with Me by Al-Saadiq Banks walks you through the seemingly dark life of Miracle, capturing the ironic circumstance of being in the wrong place at the wrong time.

Snake Eyes Mark Anthony
Keep your friends close and your enemies closer. That's the old adage in the 'hood. But what happens when your friend is your enemy? All hell breaks loose in Snake Eyes. Mark Anthony weaves a dramatic street tale that will leave you on the edge of your seat!

Cagney & Lacey Crystal Lacey Winslow
Cagney & Lacey—When two felons growing up on opposite coasts meet—the attraction is magnetic. When Lacey's past comes back to haunt her—Cagney's love is put to the test. Will Cagney ride or die for his lady? Just like a modern day Bonnie and Clyde, these two embark on a killing spree in their quest to leave the past behind.

The Deceitful Hunted Isadore Johnson
Quawi Ubati's desperation to hold on to his half billion dollar cocaine empire built by blood and fear has led him to hunt down two men responsible for the ultimate betrayal. This notorious Nigerian drug lord unleashes havoc that not even the powerful F.B.I. could withstand in order to find and kill these individuals who he once trusted before planning the ultimate escape.

Keepin' it Gangsta JM Benjamin
Keepin' it Gangsta is the only way the notorious "Dicer" knows how to live. Feared by many because of his murderous and infamous reputation—he still finds a soft spot in his black heart to hold down the only woman that ever truly loved him. But in true "Dicer" fashion he can only keep it gangsta!

ORDER FORM
(PHOTO COPY)
MELODRAMA PUBLISHING
P. O. BOX 522
BELLPORT, NY 11713-0522
(646) 879-6315
www.melodramapublishing.com
melodramapub@aol.com
Please send me the book(s):
Life, Love & Loneliness ISBN: 0-9717021-0-1

_____ @ 15.00 (U.S.) = _____
quantity

Shipping/Handling*   = _____

Total Enclosed   = _____

PLEASE ATTACH, NAME, ADDRESS, TELEPHONE NUMBER(for emergencies)

The Criss Cross ISBN: 0-9717021-2-8

_____ @ 15.00 (U.S.) = _____
quantity

Shipping/Handling*   = _____

Total Enclosed   = _____

PLEASE ATTACH, NAME, ADDRESS, TELEPHONE NUMBER(for emergencies)

Up Close & Personal ISBN: 0-9717021-1-X

_____ @ 9.95 (U.S.) = _____
quantity

Shipping/Handling*   = _____

Total Enclosed   = _____

PLEASE ATTACH NAME, ADDRESS, TELEPHONE NUMBER (for emergencies)

---

*Please enclose $3.95 to cover shipping/handling ($6.00 if total more than $30.00)
To pay by check or money order, please make it payable to Melodrama Publishing.
Send your payment with the order form to the above address, or order on the web.
Prices subject to change without notice. Please allow 4-6 weeks for delivery.
www.melodramapublishing.com